119

Hi, I'm JIMMY!

Like me, you probably noticed the world is run by adults.

But ask yourself: Who would do the best job

of making books that *kids* will love?

Yeah. **Kids!**

So that's how the idea of JIMMY books came to life.

We want every JIMMY book to be so good

that when you're finished, you'll say,

"PLEASE GIVE ME ANOTHER BOOK!"

Give this one a try and see if you agree.

(If not, you're probably an adult!)

JIMMY PATTERSON BOOKS FOR YOUNG READERS

James Patterson Presents
Sci-Fi Junior High by John Martin and Scott Seegert
Sci-Fi Junior High: Crash Landing by John Martin and Scott Seegert
How to Be a Supervillain by Michael Fry
How to Be a Supervillain: Born to Be Good by Michael Fry
How to Be a Supervillain: Bad Guys Finish First by Michael Fry
The Unflushables by Ron Bates
Ernestine, Catastrophe Queen by Merrill Wyatt
Scouts by Shannon Greenland

The Middle School Series by James Patterson
Middle School, The Worst Years of My Life
Middle School: Get Me Out of Here!
Middle School: Big Fat Liar
Middle School: How I Survived Bullies, Broccoli, and Snake Hill
Middle School: Ultimate Showdown
Middle School: Save Rafe!
Middle School: Just My Rotten Luck
Middle School: Dog's Best Friend
Middle School: Escape to Australia
Middle School: From Hero to Zero
Middle School: Born to Rock

The I Funny Series by James Patterson
I Funny
I Even Funnier
I Totally Funniest
I Funny TV
I Funny: School of Laughs
The Nerdiest, Wimpiest, Dorkiest I Funny Ever

The Treasure Hunters Series by James Patterson
Treasure Hunters
Treasure Hunters: Danger Down the Nile
Treasure Hunters: Secret of the Forbidden City
Treasure Hunters: Peril at the Top of the World
Treasure Hunters: Quest for the City of Gold
Treasure Hunters: All-American Adventure

The House of Robots Series by James Patterson

House of Robots
House of Robots: Robots Go Wild!
House of Robots: Robot Revolution

The Daniel X Series by James Patterson

The Dangerous Days of Daniel X
Daniel X: Watch the Skies
Daniel X: Demons and Druids
Daniel X: Game Over
Daniel X: Armageddon
Daniel X: Lights Out

Other Illustrated Novels and Stories

Katt vs. Dogg
Dog Diaries
Max Einstein: The Genius Experiment
Unbelievably Boring Bart
Not So Normal Norbert
Laugh Out Loud
Pottymouth and Stoopid
Jacky Ha-Ha
Jacky Ha-Ha: My Life Is a Joke
Public School Superhero
Word of Mouse
Give Please a Chance
Give Thank You a Try
Big Words for Little Geniuses
Cuddly Critters for Little Geniuses
The Candies Save Christmas

For exclusives, trailers, and other information, visit jimmypatterson.org.

MIDDLE SCHOOL
SCHOOL
BORN TO ROCK

JAMES PATTERSON

AND CHRIS TEBBETTS

ILLUSTRATED BY NEIL SWAAB

LITTLE, BROWN AND COMPANY

NEW YORK BOSTON LONDON

Copyright © 2019 by James Patterson
Illustrations by Neil Swaab
Excerpt from Katt vs. Dogg copyright © 2019 by James Patterson
Illustrations in excerpt by Anuki López
Excerpt from *Max Einstein: The Genius Experiment* copyright © 2018 by James Patterson
Illustrations in excerpt by Beverly Johnson

JIMMY Patterson Books / Little, Brown and Company
Hachette Book Group
1290 Avenue of the Americas, New York, NY 10104
JimmyPatterson.org

First Edition: February 2019

JIMMY Patterson Books is an imprint of Little, Brown and Company, a division of Hachette Book Group, Inc. The Little, Brown name and logo are trademarks of Hachette Book Group, Inc. Middle School® and the JIMMY Patterson Books® name and logo are trademarks of JBP Business, LLC.

The publisher is not responsible for websites (or their content) that are not owned by the publisher.

The Hachette Speakers Bureau provides a wide range of authors for speaking events. To find out more, go to hachettespeakersbureau.com or call (866) 376-6591.

ISBN 978-0-316-34952-9
LCCN 2018967124

10 9 8 7 6 5 4 3 2 1

LSC-C

Printed in the United States of America

MIDDLE SCHOOL
SCHOOL
BORN TO ROCK

My Name is Georgia Khatchadorian (But You Probably Already Knew That, Didn't You?)

I've wanted to be a famous rock star for a long time now. Then the other day I got my wish.

Believe it or not, I'm famous now. *Everyone* in my hometown knows who I am. In fact, it feels like everywhere you look these days—*there I am again*.

Just not in a good way.

More like a ruin-your-life, wish-you-could-crawl-in-a-hole-and-never-come-out kind of way.

And if you know anything about me and my family, then you won't be surprised when I tell you this is all my big brother Rafe's fault.

Have you ever heard the story of King Midas? He's the guy who turned everything into piles of gold just by touching it. Well, my brother is like the opposite of that. Everything *he* touches turns into huge, enormous piles of *disaster*.

Who, me?

Like, for instance, my life.

For the record, I'm not saying I'm perfect. I've made plenty of mistakes along the way, and I've had some *Titanic*-sized disasters of my very own. But none of it erases the fact that trouble follows my brother around the same way that an awful smell follows a skunk everywhere it goes.

Don't worry, I'm going to tell you all about it. But to do that, I really need to take a step back and start this story where every story starts. At the beginning.

And this one begins with a single, solitary egg.

CHAPTER 2

The Challenge

The name of the assignment was the Great Egg Drop Challenge. Our science teacher, Mrs. Hibbs, said that everyone had to design a capsule that would protect an ordinary egg from breaking when it got thrown off the roof of Hills Village Middle School.

Kind of cool, right?

For my capsule, I used a shoebox. Inside it I put a block of Styrofoam with an egg-sized hole cut out, and I tied five purple helium balloons to the outside.

Those balloons were my secret weapon. If this worked, my capsule was going to float gently down to the ground like it was made of feathers. I was

really careful about the
way I designed the whole
thing and spent a lot of time
putting it together for a few
days before it was due.

As for my brother, I
think he started his project
about ten minutes before
we had to leave for school
that morning. I could hear
him crashing around in his room while I ate my
pancakes.

"What's he doing in there?" Grandma Dotty
asked.

"Just barely scraping by," I said, because it's
true. The last time Rafe got his homework done
ahead of time was…never.

"Rafe! If you want me to drive you to school,
now's the time!" Mom yelled.

"Here I come!" he said, which is when his project
came rolling down the hall.

Have you ever seen *Raiders of the Lost Ark*?
You know that part where a giant boulder goes
tumbling after Indiana Jones and it's so big it

takes up the whole tunnel? Well, that's about what our hallway looked like just then. Except instead of a boulder, it was a giant ball made out of Bubble Wrap. Miles and miles and miles of Bubble Wrap.

"That's your egg capsule?" I said.

"When in doubt, think big!" Rafe said.

Basically, that's my brother's motto. But he also has a history of BIG-thinking his way into BIG trouble. Which is why my motto is more like, "When in doubt, do the opposite of Rafe."

"It's not even going to fit in the car," Mom said.

"That's what this is for," Rafe said, holding up some rope. "It's going on the roof."

I couldn't tell if Rafe's capsule was going to pass the challenge or if his egg would wind up like Humpty Dumpty Junior on the sidewalk. And to be honest, I didn't really care. I just wanted to get an A on my own project.

IMPORTANT FACT #1: There are some things you're going to need to know for this story. The first is that Rafe and I are in some of the same classes, even though I'm younger than him. Mom says we all have our own special talents. Being smart wasn't one of Rafe's.

But you know what else? If I'd known about the Mount Everest–sized trouble that egg was going to cause by the end of the day, I would have faked sick, stayed home, and skipped the whole thing. Too bad for me—I'm better at science than I am at seeing into the future.

So I got in the car with Mom and Rafe and headed off to school to begin the craziest, best-worst, most up-down and awful (but also awesome...but mostly awful) day of my life.

So far.

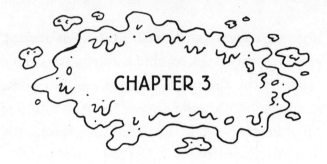

CHAPTER 3

Sam and Eggs (Get It?)

Here we go!" Mrs. Hibbs yelled from the roof of the gym. "Let the Great Egg Drop Challenge begin!"

And just like that, it started raining egg capsules.

Mrs. Hibbs sure knows how to make science class fun. She's one of my favorite teachers because of her awesome project assignments. And it was especially fun to see my own capsule touch down at about zero miles an hour. And let's just say, some of the landings weren't as graceful as mine was. I wouldn't be exaggerating if I said it honestly looked like some capsules exploded on contact.

I held my breath the whole time it took me to retrieve my shoebox, but when I looked inside, my egg was still whole, not a gloppy mess. Yes!

Mine wasn't the only one, either. About half of the eggs made it through the challenge, including Rafe's. His giant Bubble Wrap ball got the most attention when it dropped and bounced a few times, but it definitely wasn't the best capsule. The best one was Sam Marks's. He made a whole self-deploying parachute for his, which was a bit like my balloon idea, but better. And more sophisticated. And cooler.

Which brings me to...

IMPORTANT FACT #2: I have a big fat crush on Sam Marks.

Sam is the cutest boy I've ever known. He's also really nice. Nice to be around. Nice to look at. Nice to everyone he knows, including me. And it doesn't even seem like he's pretending!

We even danced at a school dance one time, but I didn't know if that meant Sam liked me the way I liked him...or not.

That's the problem with *nice*. It can mean all kinds of things!

So anyway, I was putting my capsule away after class, and Sam came right up to me at my locker.

"Hey, Georgia," he said. "Cool capsule."

"Thanks!" I said. "But yours was better. My balloons will only last for—"

"Twelve to twenty hours," he said. "I know. I thought about using them, but then I came up with the parachute instead."

I haven't even mentioned yet how smart Sam is. He's kind of a geek, but that's one of the reasons I like him. I'm kind of a geek, too. Which makes us perfect for each other. Sam probably just hasn't realized it yet.

I didn't get any closer to finding out, either. Because that's when the first really bad thing happened that day. And it was really, *really* bad— almost as if a dark, evil shadow that brought pain and suffering to everything it touched just happened to cross my path at the exact wrong moment.

And this time, I'm not even talking about Rafe.

BEWARE ALL WHO TURN THIS PAGE!

CHAPTER 4

Princesses on Patrol

That's when Missy Trillin came slithering by.

At school, Missy is the Queen of Mean. The Duchess of Darkness. The Sultan of Snobbery.

Missy makes it her full-time business to make sure everyone knows how much better she is.

"Oh, look who it is," she said. "Tell me, you two. Which came first? The geek or the egg?"

Which is when her two friends started cackling like they were at a junior witch convention. I call them the "Princess Patrol," because the princesses keep changing so there's no point in using their names. These days, Alicia and Chloe are on patrol, but Missy Trillin switches best friends the way other people change their underwear.

The thing about the Princesses is, you can't avoid them. They're just an unfortunate fact of life. Like diseases. Or tornadoes. Or that boiled vegetable medley they serve in the cafeteria.

Boy, do I hate that vegetable medley. It's like Alicia and Chloe are the mushy carrots and corn and Missy is the lima beans, which are twice as bad as both of the other two put together.

Before Sam could answer Missy's mean little joke, I glared right at her. "Buzz off, Lima Bean," I said. "We're talking here."

"Did you just call me Lima Bean?" Missy said.

The other two looked at me like I'd spat on the Queen of England. Or, at least, the Queen of Hills Village Middle School. Nobody talks to Missy that way, but I gave up worrying about her a long time ago.

Still, I probably shouldn't have made that "buzz off" comment. And I don't mean because it was rude or uncalled-for—I mean, I shouldn't have said it the same way you shouldn't poke a hornet's nest with a stick.

So there I was, standing between the nicest boy at HVMS and the meanest, most vile collection of girls on the face of the earth, not knowing what to do next, when something else came along and changed everything...*again*. I told you this was a roller-coastery kind of day, right?

Because that's when the world's coolest news hit like a ray of sunshine made out of hundred-dollar bills and unlimited Skittles.

But you're just going to have to turn the page again to find out what I mean.

I WARNED YOU **NOT** TO TURN THE PAGE! TWICE!

Best. News. Ever!

Before Missy could pounce, and before Sam could say another word, my friends Nanci, Mari, and Patti came running up the hall, grabbed me by the arm, and just kept on moving, sweeping me right along with them.

"Come with us," Mari said.

"What's going on?" I said.

"Something good," Patti said. "See you later, Sam! Georgia has to go now!"

They totally ignored the Princesses. But as we were flying away, I heard Chloe behind me.

"Why did Georgia call you Lima Bean?" she asked.

"Shut up, Chloe," Missy said.

"See you later, Georgia!" Sam called, and just like that I was gone with the wind. I mean, with the band.

IMPORTANT FACT #3: I'm in a band. Like an actual, real band. That's a big part of this story, too. It's pretty cool, but probably not as cool as it sounds. For starters, the band's name is We Stink.

Obviously, this had something to do with We Stink—but what? Whatever it was, it had to be some kind of high-security matter, because we headed straight for the bathroom. And believe me, nobody goes in there for the cozy atmosphere.

"Look at THIS!" Nanci said, as soon as the door swung shut behind us. She held up her phone and pressed Play on a video of a commercial.

"Why are you—?" I said.

"Just listen!" Mari said.

The voice in the ad said: "Okay, all you young rock stars and mock stars out there, start warming up, because Lulu and the Handbags are looking for a warm-up act."

I'm not sure what it said next, because I was too busy screaming. It was like my ears blew open, my brain caught on fire, and my stomach filled up with popping corn, all at the same time.

Lulu and the Handbags is one of my three favorite bands, and Lulu is my number one idol. She's totally cool, and talented, and she's not a supermodel or a princess or any of those other things. She's just Lulu.

And Lulu is AWESOME.

"It's open to anyone under sixteen," Nanci said. "First, you have to post a video on the contest site. Then the top twelve vote-getters will be invited to the live auditions. And the winner of that round will be the warm-up act for Lulu's big show in the city—"

"*And* win a thousand bucks!" Mari said, and we all screamed again.

To be honest, I don't like all that girly stuff, like screaming when you're excited. But for Lulu, I made an exception. If anything was worth screaming over, I'd say that a chance to meet my idol and warm up for her band was it.

This was turning out to be the best day ever!

For about another twenty seconds.

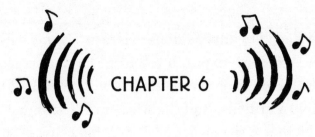

CHAPTER 6

Caught in the Act

I was just about to start watching that ad on Nanci's phone again when the bathroom door swung open.

Our principal, Mrs. Stricker, was standing right there looking at us like she'd snared four little chipmunks in her trap.

"Section three, rule two, from the Hills Village Middle School code of conduct!" Her voice echoed off the slightly slimy tiled walls. "No unauthorized cell phone usage is allowed in school except for emergencies!"

I broke in, "But Mrs. Stricker—"

"Is this an emergency?" she said.

Patti tried to get a word in. "Well—"

"No, it is not," Mrs. Stricker said. "Was there any reasonable cause for all the screaming?"

"Kind of," I said.

"No, there was not," Mrs. Stricker said.

"Are those *detention* slips?" I asked, once I saw the little pink pieces of paper in her hand.

"Yes, they are," Mrs. Stricker said. "Unless someone's hair is on fire or a wild animal has been set loose in the halls, there is *never* any reason for that kind of screaming in my school. Not to mention the cell phone."

Believe me, I know what a detention slip looks like, and it's not because I've had so many of them. It's because Rafe could wallpaper our whole apartment with the ones he's gotten.

I couldn't even argue with Mrs. Stricker. The fact was, we *had* broken the rules. Mom wasn't going to be too happy about this, either.

Rafe, on the other hand? He'd probably be proud of me.

As we came out of the bathroom, Missy and her

regal court of butt-kissers were standing right there, watching us.

"Oh, was that you in there?" Missy asked. "I thought it was a bunch of stray cats dying. So I thought I should report it to Mrs. Stricker. *Sorrr-eee!*"

"I knew it was them," Chloe said. "But I thought all that screaming was their 'band practice.'"

"How can you tell the difference?" Alicia said. "They stink!"

"It's *We* Stink," Nanci said.

"Same thing," Missy said, and the other two cracked up like Missy would immediately dump them if they didn't laugh their heads off.

I could still hear them laughing as Mrs. Stricker marched us toward the office. And all I could think about was sticking the Princess Patrol into a giant egg capsule, attaching it to a weather balloon, and sending the whole thing out over the Pacific Ocean.

Hopefully never to be seen again.

CHAPTER 7

The Detention Song

THE DETENTION SONG

Here I am, in detention,
How I got here, I hate to mention.
Something about a lip gloss queen,
Superstuck up, supermean.
She did her thing, I got in trouble,
Got a pink slip, on the double.
Now I'm trapped, I can't get out,
Man, this makes me wanna shout.
'Cause it's—
De-ten-tion!
De-ten-tion!
So many places I'd rather be,
Than in—
De-ten-tion!
De-ten-tion!
De-ten-tion!
De-ten-tion!
The clock goes tick,
The clock goes tock.
I want to leave!
I want to rock!
I'll be here until my teens.
I'll be here just like lima beans!
I hate it just like lima beans!
Hate detention, yes, it seems,
Hate it just like lima beans!
Ooh-ooh-ooh-yeah,
Hate those lima beans!
Rock out!

CHAPTER 8

A Walking Disaster

As soon as detention was over, the girls and I agreed to race home, get our stuff, and meet at the We Stink studio. Which is really just my garage.

The deadline for contest entries was coming up fast. We had to pick a song, make our video, and get it online, ASAHP (as soon as humanly possible).

So I definitely had a lot on my mind. I also had a lot in my hands, including my backpack, my lunch bag, and my egg capsule, with the egg still inside.

All of which means I wasn't paying attention to where I was going as I hurried home.

IMPORTANT FACT #4: For me, hurrying is a

little slower than it is for some people. My left leg is two centimeters shorter than my right leg. When I'm standing around with bare feet, I call myself the Leaning Tower of Georgia. I have to wear special shoes to make up the difference. My doctor says I'll probably outgrow it by the time I'm an adult. But in the meantime, I limp a little bit when I walk.

Also, my head was so full of fantasies about meeting Lulu and the Handbags, I didn't notice that I'd taken the "dangerous" way home until it was too late. And that meant I went right past the Trillin estate.

Yes, *estate.*

I'm not going to lie. Missy's family has the nicest house in Hills Village by a mile. It's surrounded by big, high gated walls, and out front there's a big statue of Major Zachary Hills. He's the founder of our town (we named it after him!), and also Missy's great-great-great-great-grandfather. Of course.

"Nice walk!" somebody yelled out.

I looked up, and it was Missy with her dog, Benjamins, coming down the driveway and out through their gate.

"Do you use that strut on the runways in Paris?" Missy asked.

And I thought, *seriously?* This girl had everything you could possibly want from the catalog of life, and she still had to make fun of the way I walked?

I know it shouldn't have hurt my feelings, because Missy is an evil troll. It doesn't seem fair that someone who doesn't have any feelings can hurt yours. But it did.

And that's probably why I snapped.

Before I knew what I was doing, I popped open that capsule of mine. I reached in. I took out my egg. And I winged it right at Missy—and made a direct hit.

"You IDIOT!" Missy screamed. "Do you know how much this T-shirt cost?"

I'm not normally the type to throw eggs at people. Even at evil people. That's more of a Rafe move than a Georgia move. But now I was going to pay a Rafe-sized price, because Missy was letting her giant Doberman off the leash and pointing him my way.

"Sic 'er, Benjamins! Eat the geek!" she said.

I may be a little slow, but I'm not bad at

climbing. So I went for the nearest high thing I could, which was the wall around the Trillin estate. It's all covered in ivy, and just like that, I was heading straight up before Benjamins could find out what I tasted like.

I also kept looking back. That was another mistake. Because at the top of the wall, there was a big concrete planter. It was the kind of thing you might look at and think, "I sure hope nobody ever bumps into that and knocks it off the wall." You might not even guess someone my size could be strong enough to do that.

But you'd be wrong.

"Watch it!" Missy screamed, just before I plowed into that planter...

...and just before it tipped right off the wall...

...and landed on top of Major Hills's statue...

...*and knocked his head clean off.*

I had just decapitated Major Hills, the village hero. Also known as Missy's great-great-great-great-grandfather. And now his head was rolling to a stop in the Trillins' driveway.

Something told me I wasn't going to make it to band practice on time.

CHAPTER 9

Head Honcho

I'd always been curious about what the inside of
the Trillins' mansion looked like. But this sure
wasn't the way I wanted to find out.

When Mom showed up, I was sitting there,
drinking water with a lemon slice in it, like I'd
been booked into the world's nicest prison.

I felt awful. I hated making trouble for Mom, just as much as I hated the way Missy kept glaring at me. You would have thought I'd declared war on all of Hills Village, starting with her family.

So when Mrs. Trillin told Mom they weren't going to make me pay for putting Major Hills's head back on, I almost wanted to kiss her. (Mrs. Trillin, I mean. *NOT* Missy.)

"Well, that's very generous," Mom said. "But I do feel as though Georgia should contribute somehow."

And that's when Missy smiled for the first time. Which made ice cubes run through my veins. Believe me, I know what makes Missy Trillin smile, and it has nothing to do with rainbows and puppy dogs.

"I have an idea," Missy said.

And I thought—

No, no, no, no, no...

"Georgia could work here until she's paid off her share," Missy said. And I thought—

No, no, no, no, no, no, no, no!

"Like as a personal assistant. I mean, *Mommy's* assistant, of course. Not mine," Missy said.

ARE YOU KIDDING ME????

I could think of a zillion things that sounded

better than this. In fact, the list was infinite, because there was *nothing* I wanted less than a prison sentence at the Trillins'.

"Well, I *could* use some help around the house a few days a week," Mrs. Trillin said.

I tried to speak up. "I don't know if that's such a good idea—"

"Excuse me?" Mom said to me, staring like I was in no position to complain. Which I wasn't. Whatever happened out there at the gate, I was the one who'd turned Major Hills into the headless non-horseman. Also, that fresh egg on Missy's shirt didn't exactly help my case.

And now Mrs. Trillin was offering us the biggest discount on statue heads anyone had ever seen.

In other words, I didn't have a choice. And just like that, I was the newest member of the Trillin estate staff.

Which also meant working for Missy.

It was like the end of the world. Only worse.

CHAPTER 10

Tick-Tick-Tick

Meanwhile...tick-tick-tick...the contest deadline was coming faster than mold on Rafe's dirty gym socks.

When the band finally got together the next day, we had less than an hour to make our video and get it online. So we just propped Nanci's phone against a paint can in the garage, turned on the camera, and stood there playing our best song. It's called "Let's Shake on It." I wrote the words and Nanci wrote the music. Hopefully it was a Lulu-worthy song, even if it was a lame video.

Either way, we got it posted to the contest site

at 4:56, with four minutes to spare. And now came the hard part.

"How are we going to get people to vote for us?" Nanci asked.

"We have to tell *everyone* we know about this," Patti said.

"It's going to take more than that," I said. "We should keep making videos, and posting pictures of the band wherever we can, with links to the voting page—"

"Who's going to see all that? We don't have any followers," Mari said.

"Then we need to get some!" I said.

"How do we do that?" Nanci asked.

"By putting up videos and pictures and…oh, wait," Mari said.

I guess that's what you call a vicious circle. How were we supposed to get people to vote for us when we didn't have any people?

"What if we played a whole bunch of shows?" I said.

"I like that," Nanci said.

"Ooh!" Mari said. "We could play free bagel Sunday at my dad's used car lot!"

"Do a lot of people come to that?" Patti asked.

"Well...no," Mari said. "But the bagels are really good."

"Maybe we could play at school," Nanci said. "Like at a pep rally or something."

"Except—" Patti looked away.

"Oh, right," Nanci said.

"Mrs. Stricker," we all said at the same time. We weren't exactly on Mrs. Stricker's best side that week. More like her worst side.

"You know what your problem is? You're not thinking big enough," one of the girls said. "Not nearly big enough."

Except, it didn't *sound* like a girl. It sounded like a boy. In fact, it sounded a whole lot like—

"Rafe!" I said. There he was, darkening my studio door. "This is a closed rehearsal. Get out!"

"I was just taking out the trash, but I couldn't help overhearing. It's like your ideas are so bad, they're hurting my ears."

"Goodbye!" I picked up my guitar. "You were just leaving."

"You shouldn't think about getting *votes*," Rafe blabbed on.

"We shouldn't?" Patti looked at him with her head cocked to the side.

"No. You should think about getting *famous*. Then the votes will take care of themselves. If you're going to do this, you might as well do it right."

But I wasn't going to listen to someone with his own permanent chair in the detention room tell me about right and wrong. Especially when that someone was Rafe.

"ONE! TWO! ONE-TWO-THREE-FOUR!" I shouted, and we started jamming out instead. I knew that would get rid of him. And it did.

"You'll be back!" Rafe yelled, even though *he* was the one running for the door. I didn't even know what he meant by that.

At least, not until later, when I figured it out the hard way.

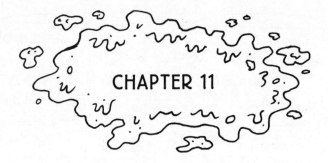

CHAPTER 11

Partners!

The next day, Mrs. Hibbs announced the new project for science.

"Does anyone know what a Rube Goldberg machine is?" she asked. We all shook our heads no, so she showed us some amazing videos.

Rube Goldberg machines usually complete a single, simple job, like turning on a light switch or opening the front door of the house or heating up a frozen pizza, but in a really crazy, complex way.

Say, for instance, you wanted to hand in your homework with a little flair.

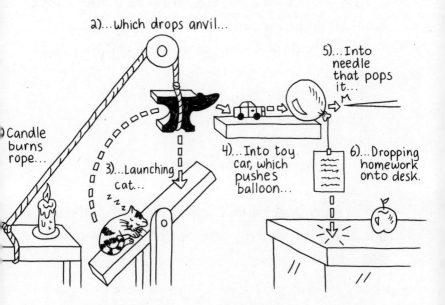

2)...Which drops anvil...

5)...Into needle that pops it...

Candle burns rope...

3)...Launching cat...

4)...Into toy car, which pushes balloon...

6)...Dropping homework onto desk.

They're made from all kinds of different stuff, and you can use whatever you can find around the house, or in the garage, or at the junk heap. They teach you about physics and engineering and creativity.

I already liked the whole idea of this assignment. And then it got even better.

"All right, everyone," Mrs. Hibbs said. "You'll be working in pairs on your machines. So please pick out a partner and get those brains storming!"

41

And guess who came straight over to me? Hello, Sam! Hello, *awesome!*

"Georgia, do you want to work on this together?" he asked.

"Sure!" I said. "That would be great."

"Cool," he said. "Because I really like—"

"I like you, too!"

"—what you did with the egg challenge."

"Oh."

I'm surprised I didn't set off the smoke alarm, because it felt like my face was on fire. Even Sam turned red.

Remember when I said how nice it would be if I could see into the future? Well, that goes double for time travel. Because I would have given anything to get a little ten-second do-over just then.

Lucky for me, Sam was extra-nice about it. He just pretended nothing had happened and kept going.

"Do you want to work on it after school?" he asked.

"Sure!" But then I remembered that I had to report to the Trillin estate at four sharp.

"Oh, wait. I can't. I have to, um…babysit, my, uh…brother."

Rafe was a few feet away, sitting there with his head upside down, trying to see something under his desk. Typical.

"Your *older* brother?" Sam asked.

"I'm not supposed to talk about it," I whispered.

I couldn't help myself. Even a crazy lie was better than admitting to Sam that Missy Trillin was my new boss.

"How about first thing next week?" Sam asked.

"That works!" I said.

"Right after school on Monday?" he said.

It was turning back to awesome, all over again. Except then I said, "Sounds like a date!"

Which is, trust me, *not* what you want to say to a boy right after you'd accidentally told him, "I LIKE YOU, TOO!" It was just like getting a do-over after all, because *now* I was just as embarrassed as I had been ten seconds earlier—if not *more* embarrassed.

But as he stood there smiling at me and I stood there smiling at him, I started to wonder if I shouldn't feel *completely* sorry for myself. Even though I probably set a world record for blushing that day, I thought that maybe Sam wasn't being nice just for the sake of being nice. And maybe he wasn't just looking for a science partner, either.

Maybe, I thought...just MAYBE...Sam Marks was starting to like me the same way I liked him. And with any luck, this new assignment was going to give me a chance to find out.

That is, if I didn't embarrass myself to death in the meantime.

First Day, Worst Day

When I rang the Trillins' doorbell that afternoon, I had one thing on my mind: HOW CAN I GET OUT OF THIS?

The short answer was: I couldn't. Not for now, anyway. The deal was for two days a week, 4:00 to 5:30, for the rest of the school year.

Still, I was going to keep my eyes, ears, and brain peeled for any possible exit strategy. Because this was 100 percent the worst thing that had ever happened to me in middle school.

And it hadn't even started yet.

"Georgia! Right on time!" Mrs. Trillin said when

she answered the door. "Come on in, I'll show you around."

She took me down a long hall, then through the enormous shiny kitchen that would've made my mom drool, a family room with at least four couches, another hall, out some French doors, and across the yard. Along the way, I saw maids in pink uniforms, a cook in a white uniform, and a couple of gardeners in green coveralls.

What I *didn't* see, thank goodness, was any sign of Missy. I'd kind of expected her to pounce the second I showed up.

Finally, we came around the corner to the swimming pool, where there was a whole other house that looked about as big as our apartment.

"Have you ever vacuumed a pool before?" Mrs. Trillin asked me.

I looked at the long pole and hose thingy she was holding out for me to take.

"Is it like vacuuming a rug?" I asked.

"Not exactly."

That pool was HUGE. Something told me I was going to be vacuuming it for the rest of the school year. But as long as I was outside and away from the Missy Danger Zone, it could have been worse.

After Mrs. Trillin showed me what to do, she handed me a little walkie-talkie with a headset. She called it a "house radio," because I guess you need that kind of thing when your property is big enough to cross state lines.

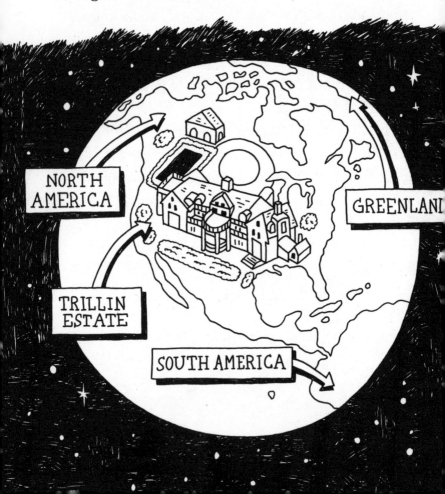

"Channel one is Nicole in the kitchen, channel two is Bobby, our head groundskeeper, and I'm on channel three," Mrs. Trillin said. "Just give a shout if you have any questions."

Then she said, "I'll leave you to it"—and disappeared back into the house.

It wasn't so bad at first. All I had to do was run the vacuum across the bottom of the pool, back and forth...and back and forth...

...and back and forth...

Before long, I was a million miles away, thinking about some day in the not-too-distant future when I'd be cleaning my *own* giant swimming pool. Because that's just the kind of internationally famous rock star I'll be. The kind who likes to keep it real.

So when Lulu and the Handbags fly in for a jam session at the studio (the one I'm going to build behind the pool house), I'll want to make sure everything is just right for them.

I mean, maybe it will be a little awkward after I beat Lulu out at the Grammys that year, but we'll work it out. Lulu's cool that way. She'll see my potential, and next thing you know, we'll be back

49

at the Grammys together, performing our mega-smash duet, "Pool Girls."

Then Lulu will score another number one hit of her own. Then I'll score another number one hit. Then Lulu. Then Georgia. Back and forth...

...and back and forth...

...and back and forth...

...and there I was, still cleaning the Trillins' pool. It was all just a nice little dream bubble while I passed the time.

And you know how it is with bubbles, right? They never last long enough.

Because this one was about to go *POP* in a major way.

Pool Girl

The first thing I heard was the sound of the pool house door opening. When I looked over, Missy's Doberman, Benjamins, came running out.

Straight at me.

I dropped my giant vacuum stick (which was a mistake, since it was the closest thing I had to a weapon) and turned to head for the main house.

Too late. He'd already caught up with me. I felt two paws on my shoulders.

"Help!" I yelled.

Benjamins knocked me down, right onto a fluffy pool chaise cushion. I tensed, waiting for those giant Doberman teeth to sink into me.

"HELLLLLP!" I tried again—just before I got a big wet lick on my cheek. And then another lick. And a third slurp that went right in my ear. I couldn't move, but only because Benjamins was giving me doggy kisses like my head was one big ice cream cone.

"Benjamins, COME!" someone said, and he jumped down.

When I looked over, you-know-who was standing there in the pool house door. The Empress of Evil herself.

"Ohhh, *sorrrr-eeee,*" Missy said. "I didn't know you were out here."

In other words, she *definitely* knew I was out there. And she'd been bluffing with Benjamins, too. Because he was no attack dog. He was just a big, scary-looking cream puff.

"Anyway," Missy said. "We're having a little study party in here, and I'm going to need you to take our snack orders."

That's when I realized how many people were inside the pool house. It wasn't just the Princess Patrol. It was more like the Princess Patrol and their whole Popular Posse, all looking at me like I was yesterday's kitchen scraps.

And today's maid.

"Your mom said I should clean the pool," I said, but Missy snatched my house radio away, turned it to channel three, and started talking.

"This is Sparkle Sparrow calling Big Bird," she said. "Mom? Come in, Mom."

The radio squawked and then I heard Mrs. Trillin.

"What is it, sweetheart?" she said. *"I'm in the middle of a pedicure—"*

"Can I borrow Georgia?" Missy said. "The pool cleaning can wait, right?"

"Yes, yes, fine," Mrs. Trillin radioed back. *"But for goodness' sake, Missy, be nice!"*

"Of *coouuurse,*" Missy said, looking at me like her definition of "nice" was the same as "evil."

Then she gave me back the radio.

"I'll have a blueberry-banana smoothie with skim milk and vanilla yogurt," Missy told me.

"Me, too," said Chloe, who had marched up behind her. "But I'm dairy-free. Soy milk for me."

"Can I get strawberry-banana but no yogurt?" Alicia asked.

"Do you have any chips?" Dexter McCourt asked. "And maybe some Zoom?"

"You know what? You'd better write this down," Missy said. "Here. You can use the back of this."

She handed me a piece of lavender stationery with some kind of long list on it. I saw lots of words like "clean" and "organize" and "perfect."

"That's my to-do list," Missy said. "Well, more like *your* to-do list now. Don't worry if you can't get to it all today. There's always the next time. Or the time after that."

The whole thing made me want to vomit in Missy's enormous pool. Except of course then I'd just have to clean that up, too.

I also wanted to cry a little. But there was no way I'd let Missy and her Popular Posse see me doing that.

Still, I didn't know what to say. If I told Missy to shove it, would she complain to her mother? And would Mrs. Trillin fire me? And would I be paying for Major Hills's head until I was eighty years old?

I really wasn't sure. Which meant I couldn't risk it.

"Oh, and one other thing," Missy said. Then Alicia came out of the pool house carrying a pink uniform on a hanger. "Make sure you put this

on before you come back with our snacks. 'Kay?
Thaaaaanks."

And that's when I started to realize just how
bad this whole thing was getting.

CHAPTER 14

Lemon Bars

I tried talking to Mom about the Missy situation that night, but there wasn't much she could do. It's not like we could suddenly afford to pay for Major Hills's head.

"You know what I'd do?" Mom said. "I'd try to focus on the positive."

"What do you mean? Like how lucky I am that Missy isn't a twin? Or how nice it is to get all that exercise running laps around the Trillin estate?"

"Nothing like that," Mom said. "You're a Khatchadorian, Georgia. We don't always have it easy in life, but we don't give up, either. Try to worry less about Missy and think more about what's been going right lately."

I couldn't argue with that, even if I kind of wanted to. So I went back to my room instead. I closed the door, opened my notebook, and tried to think about something positive. Something good in my life.

Like Lulu.

And the contest.

And We Stink's first number one hit—even if I hadn't written it yet.

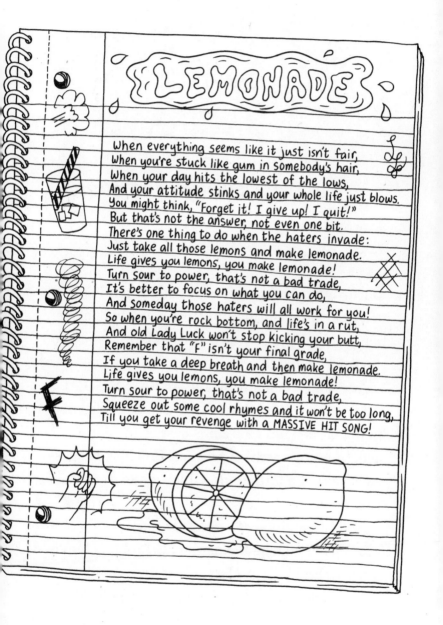

LEMONADE

When everything seems like it just isn't fair,
When you're stuck like gum in somebody's hair,
When your day hits the lowest of the lows,
And your attitude stinks and your whole life just blows.
You might think, "Forget it! I give up! I quit!"
But that's not the answer, not even one bit.
There's one thing to do when the haters invade:
Just take all those lemons and make lemonade.
Life gives you lemons, you make lemonade!
Turn sour to power, that's not a bad trade,
It's better to focus on what you can do,
And someday those haters will all work for you!
So when you're rock bottom, and life's in a rut,
And old Lady Luck won't stop kicking your butt,
Remember that "F" isn't your final grade,
If you take a deep breath and then make lemonade.
Life gives you lemons, you make lemonade!
Turn sour to power, that's not a bad trade,
Squeeze out some cool rhymes and it won't be too long,
Till you get your revenge with a MASSIVE HIT SONG!

CHAPTER 15

Our Big, Medium-Sized Break

Saturday morning, I was outside when I saw our neighbor Mrs. Gorman putting some balloons on her mailbox. There was a HAPPY BIRTHDAY sign on the front door, too.

And that's when it hit me—BRAINSTORM!

McCasalin Gorman was the closest thing our band had to a fan. She came over to the garage sometimes to watch us practice. Probably because she was in the fifth grade, which made us at least a little bit cool to her.

And I thought—*why didn't I come up with this before?* Hills Village Elementary School had hundreds of fourth and fifth graders. What if we could turn every single one of them into a vote for We Stink?

I hated to admit it, but Rafe was right. We needed to think *big*. If we could crack the birthday party circuit, we were going to be one giant step closer to winning this whole thing.

"Hi, Mrs. Gorman," I said, like I just happened to be walking by. "I see you're having a party. How would you like some free live music? My band had a cancellation this morning, so we're available."

"Really?" she said. "Do you play music that's appropriate for children?"

"Sure!" I said. Which was true. We're not exactly a parental advisory lyrics kind of group.

"Well, that would be wonderful," she said. "I was supposed to have Shrimpy the Clown, but apparently he picked up a case of head lice at his last party, so…can you be ready in an hour?"

"Of course we can!" I said.

I thought it was a little weird for McCasalin to want a clown at her birthday, but it didn't matter now. Shrimpy's bad luck was our big break. I turned around and ran home to call the girls and get ready.

We were going to need our instruments, of course. Also Nanci's phone, for filming purposes. And something to tell people about the contest. So right after I called Mari and told her to call Patti and Nanci, I made the

VOTE FOR
WE STINK!

Go to
www.LuluContest.com/WeStink!

world's quickest flyer on Mom's computer. It wasn't great, but I didn't have time for *great*.

"What are you doing?" Rafe asked me.

"See? I can think big," I said, and handed him one of the flyers. "We're going to get every fourth and fifth grader in Hills Village to vote for us."

"Wow," Rafe said.

"Thanks," I said.

"No," he told me. "It's more like I'm starting to feel sorry for you."

"Here's an idea," I said, and snatched the flyer out of his hand. "Don't bother me about it."

It was stupid to even try and have a real conversation with Rafe. Not to mention a waste of my time. I had to get busy launching the VOTE FOR WE STINK campaign, once and for all.

"I'm just saying—"

"La-la-la-la-la-la!" I said to Rafe, as I picked up my stuff and flew back out the door. "Not listening!"

"Yeah," I heard my brother say behind me. "That's pretty much your problem, right there."

Change of Plans

Okay, in my defense, I want to say that what happened next could have happened to anyone. It was all just a misunderstanding.

When I got back to the Gormans' house, Mrs. Gorman had her hands full. She was carrying around McCasalin's baby brother, and he was crying up a storm, so she just pointed me toward the backyard and kept moving.

Nanci was already there, setting up her drums. Patti and Mari were on the way. And the whole house smelled like cake.

As soon as I saw McCasalin, I went right over to her. She was our ticket to the rest of Hills Village Elementary, so I wanted to be especially nice and get her pumped for our show.

"Hey, McCasalin!" I said. "Happy birthday! That's a nice jacket! Did you get it as a gift?"

But McCasalin looked at me like I was speaking some kind of secret language. A bunch of other adults were just getting there, too. And the weird part was, they all had babies and toddlers with them.

"It's not *my* birthday," McCasalin said.

"Wait…what?" Mari said. She and Patti had just gotten there, too. Now everyone was staring at me.

"It's Adam's birthday," McCasalin told me, and pointed at her one-year-old brother. "I hope you guys know 'Itsy Bitsy Spider,' because that's his favorite."

"Hey, sweetie!" Mr. Gorman yelled from a car in the driveway. "The movie starts in twenty minutes. Let's roll!"

"Catch you next time!" McCasalin said, and took off, just like that.

I didn't even think about giving her a flyer until she was already gone. I was too busy noticing the way Mari, Patti, and Nanci were looking at me—like I had one big *"OOPS!"* tattooed across my forehead.

So basically, the first show of our big campaign didn't go quite as planned. I mean, we did end up with a houseful of screaming babies, but I don't think that had anything to do with the music.

Let's just say it gave our band name a whole new meaning. And not in a good way.

Mixed Messages

After that disaster, I was really looking forward to Monday after school. That's when I had my first maybe-date with Sam. And, boy, was it *romantic*. We went to the junk shop, the city dump, and the hardware store, looking for parts for our Rube Goldberg machine.

"What about this?" Sam asked, picking up a giant spring at the junk shop. "Maybe we could use it to trigger a catapult."

"And then have it toss a ball into this," I said, holding up an old butterfly net. "That could be cool."

I know, I know. Not exactly romantic. But most

of the couples I know in middle school don't even get past holding hands in the hall between classes. At least we were off school grounds.

See, I still hadn't figured out if Sam and I were friends, or more than friends, or just plain old science partners and nothing more. But it's like Mom said: "Khatchadorians don't give up easily." So while we looked for machine parts, I also tried to look for clues.

"This is all so time-consuming," I said, as casually as I could. "I wonder how real scientists find time for other stuff."

"What other stuff?" Sam asked.

"Oh, I don't know," I said. "Like having a social life. Going on dates. Or whatever."

In other words: HINT HINT HINT HINT HINT.

"Hmm," Sam said, as he picked up a rusty old hinge from one of the twenty-five-cent bins.

Just "hmm." *That was it.*

It's possible he'd gotten my drift, and maybe he was just too shy to do anything about it. But it was also entirely possible that a bin of old rusty hinges was more interesting to Sam Marks than I could ever hope to be. The point is, I had no idea.

In a perfect world, middle school boys would come equipped with a button you could press to make them tell you exactly what they were thinking at any time. But of course this isn't a perfect world.

Maybe what I really needed was a whole new kind of machine—one that would get me an A in science, a Nobel Prize, and maybe, just maybe, a boyfriend, all at the same time.

But you know what they call that, right?

Wishful thinking.

DON'T EVEN THINK ABOUT IT
JUST FRIENDS
LUKE WARM
LUKE WARMER
GETTING THERE
CRUSH-O-RAMA
HOT FOR YOU
GEORGIA, WILL YOU BE MY GIRLFRIEND???

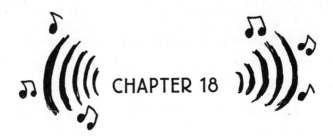

CHAPTER 18

Worse Than I Thought

So if my Monday with Sam was a C-plus, then my Tuesday was more like an F. Unless there's such a thing as an F-minus.

There I was, minding my own business at school, when Missy's friend Alicia came right up to me in the hall and held out this little bag.

"I need these washed by tomorrow," she told me. "Missy said you could take care of it for me at her house this afternoon."

At first I thought Alicia must be joking. But then I remembered that the one accessory Princesses *don't* come with is a sense of humor.

"Are you seriously trying to give me your laundry?" I asked.

"Don't be ridiculous," Alicia said.

"Good," I said. "Because there's no way—"

"It's just a few delicates that need hand-washing," she said. "If I was giving you my laundry, it would be a much bigger bag."

I think Alicia actually expected me to take it. But instead, I told her where she could stick her delicates and sent her on her way.

"You haven't heard the end of this," she said.

"Whatever," I said.

About ninety seconds later, I had a face full of Missy Trillin. She came right up to me in the cafeteria.

"If I want you to wash my friends' clothes, then you're going to wash my friends' clothes," she said.

I could feel my face turning red. People were starting to stare. I wished I had a dozen fresh eggs to throw at Missy. That would give her some laundry, all right!

But lucky for me, there weren't any eggs on

hand, and I couldn't afford another punishment. So I just told her the same thing I'd told Alicia, except I gave her the spicier version. Let's just say it was somewhere north of PG-13.

And then I walked away while Missy steamed and stewed.

It felt pretty good, to be honest. But it was also only like winning a teeny-tiny battle in the middle of a ginormous war. Because I knew for a fact that Alicia's handwashables were going to be waiting for me when I got to the Trillins' that afternoon, like it or not.

In other words, I wasn't just working for one evil troll now. I was working for *all* of them.

And the only thing I could do in the meantime was make sure Missy never got to see just how badly she was driving me CRAZY.

What's the Big Idea?

After four days online, We Stink's video was barely getting any votes at all. So far we were in forty-eighth place. Out of fifty-one entries.

And I'm not even sure the other three were real bands.

48) We Stink!

49) Asdfghjkl;

50) Ura Nidiot

51) [System Error: 404]

KEEP THOSE VOTES COMING IN!

Lulu AND THE HANDBAGS

Tweet   Share

I was starting to feel the pressure, big-time. Between this impossible contest and my impossible prison sentence at the Trillin estate, not to mention my homework and guitar practice, it was starting to feel a little head-explodey, if you know what I mean.

But if there's one thing I'm not, it's a quitter. (Actually, there are lots of things I'm not, like popular, or pretty, or rich. But the point is—I wasn't giving up yet.)

"The voting period is only two weeks," Mari said that afternoon at band practice. "I don't think we're going to make it."

"Come on," I said. "We still have a week and a half to get into the top twelve! We can do this!"

The truth is, nobody loves Lulu and the Handbags more than I do. Which I think meant nobody wanted this more than I did. And maybe that's why I was doing most of the work so far.

"We're going to have to pull off something drastic," Nanci said.

"Something big to get people's attention," Patti said.

"Something *really* big," Mari said.

And that's when my next idea hit me—
hard. Let's call it the World's Most Unwanted
Brainstorm. It was like a giant gift that came
wrapped in barbed wire and poison dart frogs, with
signs that said DANGER!, KEEP OUT!, and DON'T EVEN
THINK ABOUT IT!

Except I *was* thinking about it. Because the
truth is, my brother knows how to think big. And
getting attention is one of Rafe's specialties.

So I waited until after practice. Then I went
inside.

I took a deep breath.

I crossed my fingers.

I crossed my toes.

And I slowly walked toward the point of no
return…the brink of disaster…the entrance to the
Dangerous One's Lair…

Also known as Rafe's door.

CHAPTER 20

Crossing Over to the Dark Side

So in other words," Rafe said five minutes later, "you're willing to do my homework for the rest of the year if I help you?"

"Uh…*no*," I said. "Were you even listening?"

"Oh, I was listening all right," he said. "And all I heard was the sweet sound of desperation."

I knew this was a bad idea. But now it was too late to turn around. Not until I gave it my best shot.

"Listen," I told him, "this contest comes with some prize money—"

"Prize money?" he said. Now he looked

interested, like I'd dangled a giant hot-fudge-and-dollar-bill sundae in front of him. "How much are we talking about?"

"My share would be two hundred fifty—"

"Done!" Rafe said. "You can start your internship by getting me a can of Zoom and a bag of chips from the kitchen. Or you can run to the store, if we're all out. Which we probably are."

I took another deep breath. Something told me I was going to be taking a lot of those for the next week and a half. But if I just imagined Lulu waiting for me at the end of that long, dark tunnel, I could make it through anything.

In fact, now that I had something Rafe wanted on the table, we could really get down to business.

"Slow down a second," I told him. "I have a few conditions of my own. First of all, I'm not doing anything illegal or against the rules."

"Yawn," Rafe said.

"Two. If we don't win, you don't get anything."

"No problem," he said. "I live for risk."

"Three. You have to give me a free sample first."

"Free sample? What does that mean?" he said.

"One really good idea."

"I can do that," he said.

"And, four," I told him, "the girls can't know we have a deal. They have to think that whatever you're coming up with is coming from me."

"Huh?" Rafe said.

"This is my band. My deal. My contest," I said. "And I intend to keep it that way."

And yeah, I was totally bluffing. But there was no reason to roll over and play dead from the start.

For a minute, Rafe sat there and thought about it. Actually, he was probably just thinking about what he could buy with two hundred fifty dollars, but I played along.

"Okay," he said finally. "You've already admitted that you need me, and that I'm the king of good ideas. I guess I can live with the rest."

I took one more long, deep breath. This was what you might call a choose-your-battles moment.

"What about my free sample?" I asked.

"Already got it," Rafe told me. "I'm way ahead of you."

Then he picked up his sketchbook and scribbled something really fast.

"Here you go," he said, and turned the pad around to show me. "It's just a start, but I think you're going to like it."

And I'm not going to lie. I kind of loved it.

Reality Check

I got right to work after that and did something I should have done a long time ago. I put We Stink online.

You didn't think I was leaving it *all* up to Rafe, did you? I'm not that crazy.

I started with Instagram, Snapchat, Twitter, Facebook, and Google+ accounts. Then I set up We Stink channels on YouTube and Vimeo. I made us a Wikipedia page, too, and submitted it for review. I might have exaggerated a tiny bit for that, but what can I say? Rafe had me thinking LARGE.

WIKIPEDIA

We Stink: The World Tour

We Stink is in the launch phase of its first-ever world tour, bringing cutting-edge music and vocals to their fans (We Stinkers) around the globe. First stop—Hills Village. Next up, who knows? Rome...Beijing... London...Honoluli...

Contents

1)
2)
3)

Vote for We Stink here!!!

History

Shredder

The Key-master

Lo Lo

Sticks

No, really—VOTE RIGHT NOW!

After that, I went online and found a list of 122 other social media websites. That was like 122 different ways of getting more votes.

And no, I didn't sign up for all of them. Just Blogger, Reddit, Tumblr, Pinterest, LinkedIn, LiveJournal, Digg...

...Skype, Snype, Periscope, Meerkat, Pitter, Patter, Smatter, Smatter2, Pic-A-Boo...

...X-Wow, Band-O-Rama, Twoo, Zing, Wing, Bing—

"GEORGIA!"

All of a sudden, Mom was in my room.

"Huh?" I said.

When I looked up, she was standing there in her bathrobe. The clock on my laptop said 1:34 a.m., and my eyelids felt like they had tiny dumbbells pulling them closed.

"What are you doing up so late?" Mom asked.

"I guess I lost track of time."

"Is this about the Lulu contest?" she said. "Sweetie, I don't want you getting carried away."

I was going to say, "I'm not getting carried away!" But since I'd just spent the last ten minutes signing up for a Slovakian music newsletter, maybe it was time to call it a night.

"The thing is, we only have ten days to get into the top twelve," I said. "I have to make sure people notice us, or I'll never meet Lulu!"

Mom came over and sat on my bed.

"Let me ask you something," she said. "If you could ask Lulu *one* question, what would it be?"

I had about eighteen thousand questions for Lulu. But if I could only ask one—

"I'd want to know what it's like to walk onstage with thousands of people screaming your name," I said.

"You wouldn't ask about the music?" Mom said. "Or the writing process?"

"You said just one question," I said.

She took my laptop and put it on the desk, and started to tuck me in like when I was little.

"I think you should worry more about what kind of musical artist you'd like to be," she said, "and maybe a little less about getting famous."

Mom's all about the art. She's a painter, and creates these really cool abstracts.

But at the same time, I'm not so sure she knows what it's like to be my age. I mean, no offense to

Mom, but she didn't even go to middle school in this century.

"We do rock and roll," I said. "Not art."

"What do you think songs are? They're poems and music," she said. "And you're so good with words. It doesn't have to be big and heavy. It just has to come from you."

"But that doesn't mean people will like it," I said.

"I'd say it's better to lose as yourself than to win as someone else," she said, and gave me a kiss good night. "Think about it."

And I would. My mom's pretty smart. But meanwhile, that didn't mean I was going to slow down on the other stuff.

Oh, no.

No, no, no, no, no.

The World Tour was still very much ON.

CHAPTER 22

Let's Go to the Movies

When I came into the kitchen for breakfast the next morning, Rafe had his hands held up like this.

"Miss Khatchadorian!" he said. "Today is the first day of shooting on your new movie. How does it feel?"

"It feels like I just woke up and you're already being weirder than usual," I said.

"Cut!" Rafe said, and put his hands down. "I'm just practicing. Because I had an even bigger idea last night."

"Bigger than We Stink: The World Tour?" I asked.

Rafe held up his hands again. "Get this," he said. "We Stink: The World Tour: *A Rock-You-Mentary*." Then he put down his hands and looked at me. "Get it? Like a *documentary* about a *rock* band on their way to the top."

I was actually impressed. And even a tiny bit touched.

"Do you really think we can win this thing?" I asked.

"Probably not," he said. "But I'll bet Mrs. Donatello will give me credit for art class, either way."

I might have guessed.

"Flip said I could use his camera," Rafe went on. "He's got a GoBro, too. Those things are sweet! This movie's gonna be killer!"

GO BRO
THE CAMERA DUDES LOVE

"I can't afford to pay Flip, too," I said. "You'll have to share any prize money you get with him—"

"Flip's not in it for the money," Rafe said. "He has a crush on, like, half of We Stink, so basically, he's on board for anything."

"Hang on," I said. "Flip has a crush? On which half?"

"Well," Rafe said, "it's more like he *used* to think you were cute—"

"He WHAT?"

"—but I talked him out of that," Rafe said. "Now he likes Mari. And it wouldn't kill you to let her know that, by the way."

I was still stuck on the part about how Flip Savage used to think I was cute. Even if he didn't think so anymore.

I mean, it's not like I WANTED Flip to like me. The idea of going out with my brother's best friend was kind of gross. And for another thing, I liked Sam.

But still, this was good news. Because if I could be completely clueless while Flip thought I was cute, then maybe it was also possible for Sam to like me without my ever figuring it out.

That was a big maybe, but even so—

"Hello? Earth to Georgia?" Rafe waved a hand

in front of my face. "Do you want to talk about this movie idea or not?"

"Definitely," I said, snapping to attention. "So when do we start?"

"As soon as we get to school. And this afternoon, you need to get your band to City Hall Park for your first music video shoot."

Okay, I'll admit it. Rafe was on a roll.

There was only one problem.

"I can't this afternoon," I said. "I have to work at the Trillins'."

Rafe gave me this look, like I was the world's leading cause of lameness.

"What?" I said. "It's not like I'm doing volunteer work over there!"

"The day after tomorrow, then," he said. "No excuses."

Already, my brain was bubbling with ideas. But I didn't want to get *too* excited yet. This was Rafe, after all.

"I'm in," I said. "Just don't mess it up, okay?"

"What makes you think I'm going to mess anything up?" he asked.

If I could have, I would have handed him a copy of his own life story to make my point.

"Just remember, you work for me," I said.

"I don't think of it like that," Rafe said. "It's more like you're the engine, but I'm the gas." And just to prove it, he let one rip right there at the breakfast table.

Yeah. Because nothing inspires confidence like a game of Pass the Gas from the kid who's taking your entire future into his own hands.

Hoo, boy. What had I just gotten myself into?

CHAPTER 23

Scene One

And...ACTION!"

"I can't be-*LIEVE* that *WE* are on our *WAY* to the *TOP!*" Nanci said to me while we opened our lockers.

"CUT!"

We both stopped and looked at Rafe.

"What is it now?" Nanci asked.

We'd been working on our Rock-You-Mentary for five minutes, and Mr. Big Shot Director was already getting on our nerves.

"People are staring," I said. "Do we really have to do this in front of everyone?"

"Right," Rafe said. "Because doing this where people *won't* notice is a great way of getting famous."

I'd already gotten at least five eye rolls, although one of those might have just been Ashley Catalan's allergies acting up. Still, I felt like a fish in a fishbowl under a microscope.

But Rafe was right. If I wanted to be famous, I was going to have to suck it up and get used to it. And middle school is all about learning to be the adults we're going to be, right?

"Okay, let's do it again," I said. Right before we got slammed by a Princess hit-and-run.

"Oh, *wow!*" Missy Trillin said, oozing by in a strawberry-scented cloud. "That…is…*adorable.*"

Chloe and Alicia were there, too, of course. It's like Missy keeps them on invisible leashes.

"I wouldn't shoot more than one episode of that little reality show," Chloe said. "It's going to be canceled before it starts."

"It's not a reality show!" Mari said. "It's a documentary."

"It's a *Rock*-You-Mentary," Rafe said.

"Awwww," Missy said. "That's even more

adorable. You know—in a sad, pathetic kind of way."

"Who do you guys think you're fooling?" Alicia said. "You're just a middle school band—"

"Yeah," Chloe said. "Band of losers!"

Then someone else chimed in.

"You're the ones talking about them," Sam said. "I don't see them worrying about what *you're* up to."

I hadn't even seen him coming. He just showed up like some kind of superhero. You know, the kind with an armful of books and a ketchup stain on his hoodie.

But he was *my* superhero.

Missy and her prissy minions didn't even have a good comeback. Or anything to say for that matter.

But Mrs. Stricker sure did.

"EXCUSE ME!" she said. "Am I the only one who heard the first-period bell? Rafe, put that camera away!"

"We're making a documentary," he said. "It's for art."

"Ten, nine, eight..." she said.

"You can ask Mrs. Donatello!" Rafe said.

"Seven, six, five..."

"We're going!" I said, and we scattered before Mrs. Stricker could get anywhere near three, two, one. I didn't want to find out what came after that.

The Princesses scattered, too. I could hear them on their way to class.

"Did you study for the math test?"

"There's a math test?"

"Exactly."

"No, seriously, there's a test...?"

That was the last I heard before I stopped worrying about them and started thinking about other stuff instead. Like my science project.

And by science project, of course, I mostly mean *Sam*.

Science Experiment

So if the tin can with the golf ball tips over here," Sam said, putting it next to an old piece of wooden train track, "the golf ball can run down the track, and knock the marble into the funnel—"

He flicked the marble into the funnel, where it spiraled around, then down through the hole—

"And onto the Return button on my laptop," I said. "Which I'll have preset to text Swifty's Diner."

Everyone in the class was using marbles and tracks and pendulums for their machines, too. But no one was making a robocall-the-diner, order-your-breakfast, and have-it-waiting-for-pickup-on-the-way-to-school…machine.

The problem was, every time that marble plopped out of the funnel, it just rolled across my keyboard and hit the floor with a dull clunk. It was like the sound of a C-minus, if you know what I mean.

"Hmm," Sam said. "Maybe we need a heavier marble."

"By the way," I told him, "thanks for standing up for us in the hall like that."

"No prob," he said, and went back to looking at the assignment sheet, while I just looked at him.

I'd been trying to figure Sam out for forever now. I talked it over with Mari, Patti, and Nanci, and they all thought that even though he hadn't asked me on a date, he liked me. And to be honest, so did I. But I needed some proof, and everything I tried just went *clunk,* like that marble on the floor.

But Mrs. Hibbs always says if your experiment isn't working, try coming at it from a different angle.

So I did.

"So, we've been working on some new songs for the band," I said.

"Cool," Sam said, and tore off a piece of duct tape.

"Yeah," I said. "The new one's called 'Do You Like Me Like That?'"

"Uh-huh," he said, taping the funnel into place.

"We also have one called 'What Are You Doing Saturday Night?'" I said. "Because I was thinking we could do something together. You know—just the two of us."

"Awesome," he said. He didn't even look up. Seriously, this boy was cute, smart, nice, and CLUELESS.

And I was running out of ideas.

CHAPTER 25

#DoYouLikeMeLikeThat?

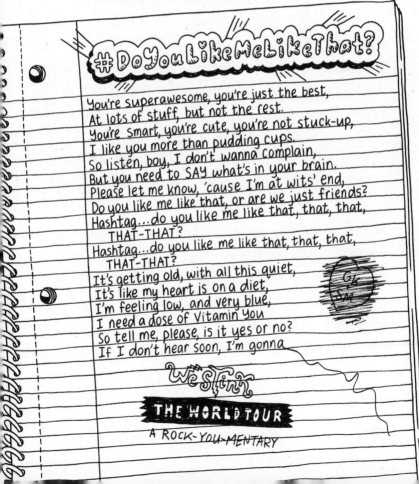

"Whatcha doin'?" Rafe asked. "Is that a new song?"

When I looked up, he was pointing his camera right at my notebook. I practically jumped eight feet, but not as fast as I slammed that notebook closed.

"NO! WHY WOULD YOU ASK THAT? IT'S PRIVATE. DID YOU SEE ANYTHING?" I said.

"Wow," Rafe said, "who put the Red Bull in your chocolate milk?"

"Nobody!" I said. "I mean…just let me know next time you point that thing at me. There's a fine line between making a movie and snooping, you know."

"Not when you're a celebrity," he said.

"I'M NOT A CELEBRITY!" I yelled.

Which was unfortunate, since I was sitting in the corner of the cafeteria. And now everyone was probably wondering why I thought I needed to announce that to the world.

If I ever do get famous, something tells me it's going to be a lot harder than it looks.

Thanks a lot, Rafe.

CHAPTER 26

Two to Tutor

When I got to the Trillins' that day, things with Missy got worse in a whole *new* way.

"Georgia!" Mrs. Trillin said. "Come in. I need to ask you a favor."

And I thought, what now? Oil change for the limo? Polish the burglar alarms? But that wasn't even close.

"I understand you do fairly well in school, is that right?" she asked me.

"I guess," I said. I didn't want to brag.

"Well, Melissa's math test did *not* go well," she said. "And I'm insisting that she get a tutor. So I thought as long as you're here—"

I kind of gasped. Or at least gulped.

"Excuse me?" I said. "You want me to…to…tu…."

"Tutor Missy," Mrs. Trillin said. "That's right."

And I thought—well, that's the worst idea since meatless bacon. It was bad enough working for the Princess Patrol, but tutoring would mean I had to spend every minute of my prison sentence in the same room as Missy. No, thank you!

"I don't mean to be rude, Mrs. Trillin, but you know we're not exactly friends, right?" I said.

"But, sweetheart, Missy *asked* for you," she said.

Oh. My. *Geometry.* It was even worse than I thought. This was like being invited into the alligator pit by the head alligator herself.

The question was, what torture did Missy have in mind for me now?

"I guess she knows how smart you are," Mrs. Trillin said. "Also, she needs to earn a B or better on the next quiz if she wants to get *this* back."

Then she held up a cell phone in a familiar lavender leather case.

"Ohhhh," I said. It all started adding up in my mind like…well, like a big math problem.

FACT #1: I didn't really have a choice about the tutoring. I basically had to do what Mrs. Trillin said.

FACT #2: Missy didn't really have a choice, either. Not if she wanted her phone back. (And Missy *definitely* wanted her phone back. She loved that thing more than water, air, and lip gloss combined.)

FACT #3: That meant I had something Missy needed. Also known as math skills. Which was like having Missy's fate in my hands.

"I'd be happy to help out," I said.

"Wonderful!" she said. "She's just up in her room, pouting."

(Did I mention that I was starting to like Mrs. Trillin?)

"Actually, is there a bathroom I could use first?" I asked.

I didn't really have to go. I just needed a minute to figure out what I was going to do next.

Because now, it was like I had the alligator by the jaws. That's better than the other way around, but it's also dangerous. I needed to proceed with extreme caution.

One thing was for sure, though. Opportunity had just knocked, and I intended to answer the door.

Missy — Phone + Math x Georgia = ?????

Missy's bedroom was just as megasized as I'd expected. She had a canopy bed that was about two stories high, and a whole media center with *two* TVs. Why two? Is she afraid she'd miss out on the latest toothpaste commercial?

There was also a spiral staircase going up to a loft, with a window that looked out toward the pool house. I could live in that room and still have space for a live elephant collection.

Meanwhile, Missy was laid out on her bed like a starving castaway on a tiny, fluffy island.

I've heard that humans can last for three weeks without food, three days without water, and three minutes without oxygen. But when I got there, it looked like Missy wasn't going to make it another three seconds without that phone.

"What are you waiting for?" she said. "Let's get this over with. And you'd better be a good teacher."

"Actually," I said, "we have a little business to attend to first."

"What's *that* supposed to mean?" she said.

I stepped inside and closed the door.

"Here's the deal," I said. "I'm going to get you a B or better on that quiz. But first you're going to talk to your mom about getting me out of this whole servant deal once you pass."

Missy looked at me like I was a piece of gum stuck to her shoe.

"You can't talk to me like that," she said. "You work for me."

"Okie-dokie," I said, and turned to leave. "I'm sure you'll be just fine using your desktop and land line for the rest of the year—"

"Wait!"

I stopped with my hand on the doorknob. And that's when my house radio squawked to life.

"How's it going up there, girls?" Mrs. Trillin said. *"Do you have everything you need?"*

I picked up to answer and said, "Actually, Mrs. Trillin, I'm not sure this is going to—"

Right before Missy flew across the room on her broomstick and snatched the radio out of my hand.

"We're *greeeaaat!*" she told her mom, in her fakest, most princessy voice. "I'm getting smarter already. Aren't I, Georgia?"

"I don't know," I said. *"Are you?"*

Missy gave me a super-glare then. The kind that could wilt flowers. And probably set them on fire, too.

"Mommy, I'm coming downstairs," she said into the radio. "I need to talk to you about something first."

Then she shoved the radio back in my hand.

"Satisfied?" Missy asked.

"Actually," I said, "I could really use one of those fruit smoothies, too. Maybe pick it up on your way back?"

Missy gave me another evil look. But then she headed for the door.

"Just so we're clear," she said, "I hate you."

"Strawberry-banana would be just *greeeeaaat!*" I said. "Thanks!"

In other words, mission accomplished.

I guess maybe Rafe and I are a little bit alike, after all.

Shopping!

I was in a pretty good mood by the time I got home, even if tutoring Missy was like one of those bad dreams where you keep ending up in the same place, over and over and over....

But at least there was an end in sight. Mrs. Trillin agreed to end my prison sentence if Missy got a good grade on her quiz!

To celebrate, I scooted out to meet the girls for a little bargain shopping.

If we were going to shoot a real-live music video the next day, we wanted to look like real-live rock stars.

For about ten bucks apiece, if at all possible.

Lucky for us, Patti knew about an awesome thrift store called New2U, where we went crazy trying stuff on. So by the time we were done, we went from this...

♡ ◎
22 likes
WeStink #beforeshot #LuluContest #VoteForWeStink!
#PleeeeeeeeaseVoteForWeStink!
#noreallydoitnow

to this...

And finally, because the lady at the counter said they were closing and we had to pick something, we ended up with this.

Not bad, right?

"Do we look like rock stars?" Mari asked.

"I guess so," I said.

"But now we need to start *acting* like rock stars," Nanci said. So we trashed the store and left without paying.

Just kidding. We cleaned up after ourselves, paid, thanked the clerk, and left.

But you can bet we looked ROCKIN' AWESOME doing it.

CHAPTER 29

A Lean, Clean Music Machine

The next day was the first official stop on the We Stink World Tour. I went straight from school with my guitar to meet the girls by Millennium Fountain in City Hall Park.

It was a good location. The fountain had all these splooshy jets of water that made a really good backdrop for our video. I was getting excited.

"How is this any different from the last two times we played here?" Mari asked. "We didn't get applause then. We got crickets!"

I tried to stall, since I didn't exactly know. "Well…"

"We're here! We're here!" Rafe said, just in time. He'd brought Flip, too.

"Hey, everyone," Flip said. And then, "Hi, Mari."

"Hey, Flip," Mari said, smiling, and you could just practically see their eyes turning into hearts like those emojis. Which was fine with me, because Flip was here to help. And the more people around, the better.

"What's in the backpack?" Nanci asked him.

"Oh, just some of Rafe's awesome flyers," Flip said, and pulled out a handful. They had the World Tour logo on them, along with a link for our voting page.

"Rafe's going to film, you guys are going to play, and I'm going to hand these out to people," Flip said.

"Okay, let's do this!" Rafe said.

"Do *what*, exactly?" I asked.

"You four just stand there and play. We'll take care of the rest," he said. "And no matter what happens, *don't stop*."

That's when I started getting the creepy, tingly feeling up the back of my neck. I call it the Rafe Alarm. It's when you know something's wrong, and you know it's Rafe's fault, but you just don't know what it is yet.

"What's that supposed to mean?" I asked, right before Nanci counted us off. We'd chosen one of our rockingest songs, "Spring Cleaning," so I didn't have any choice but to start playing.

At first, a bunch of people looked over, just like the last time we played City Hall Park.

And then they all went back to ignoring us. Just like the last time. I noticed Flip had disappeared, too. Maybe even *he* was bored.

"Nothing's happening!" I told Rafe, right into the camera.

"Just give it a second," he said.

And then, sure enough…people started noticing again. Some of them came closer. Others were pointing.

It was working! Our music was hooking the crowd. Maybe Mom was right, after all, I thought. We *were* musical artists! And if I just kept focusing on my writing, then everything else would take care of itself.

Except—that's when I noticed the bubbles.

Lots and lots of soapy bubbles were filling up the fountain behind me. It looked like the world's biggest washing machine had gone berserk. And the pile was getting bigger, fast.

But so was the crowd.

"What did you do?" I asked Rafe with my back turned to everyone.

"Just go with it!" he said. Then he stuck the camera

in my face, swooped away, and got a shot of Nanci at the drums, right before the song came to an end.

"Again!" Rafe yelled. "One! Two! One-two-three-four!"

"That's my job!" Nanci said.

"Whatever! Keep playing!" he said.

The suds were spilling right out of the fountain by now. And some of the kids were climbing right in. The more they kicked around, the higher that mountain got, and the more it spilled around our feet and ankles. Pretty soon, it looked like We Stink was rocking out on top of a giant whipped-cream-covered sundae.

Three words: Awe. Some. Ness.

It was insane! In the most tremendously, awesomely bubblicious possible way.

I was still a little freaked out about how this got started, and whether we were going to get in trouble, but then the Channel 12 News van pulled up. A reporter jumped out with a cameraman behind her and they headed right for us.

It was amazing how fast they'd gotten there. I guess *someone* must have called ahead and tipped them off.

Imagine that.

Time to throw out the things I don't need.
But the one thing I don't need to keep is you!
Woof!
12

CHAPTER 30

Tonight's Top Story

We had to rush home to catch the evening news, and we got there just in time.

"Turn on the TV, turn on the TV!" I said to Grandma Dotty, who was home while Mom was at work.

And then there we were.

"Good evening, I'm Carly Morehead and these are tonight's top stories. A local band's performance in City Hall Park today was interrupted by a gigantic bubble bath...."

"Hashtag omigosh!" I said. It was happening. I was on TV!

"I know that girly!" Grandma Dotty said, and hugged me really tight.

Meanwhile, Rafe was filming me while I was watching. "Sit closer to the TV," he said. "And look over here!"

"SHHH!" I said, because my interview with the reporter was just coming on.

When she interviewed me at the park, I told her all about the World Tour and the Lulu contest, and I must have said "Vote for We Stink" about twenty times.

But all they showed was a tiny little clip with my name misspelled.

That was it. But even so, it was the most famous I'd ever been. By a long shot.

As soon as the story was over, the phone rang. It was Mari calling to scream about how amazing it all was. Rafe said he was going to run over to her house and "do an on-the-spot interview."

Then the phone rang again, and it was Nanci. Everything was moving so fast!

When the doorbell rang a minute later, I thought maybe it was Patti. Or maybe another reporter. Or maybe…

Then I looked out the front window.

Some kind of official-looking car was parked outside. Not only that, but an official-looking man in an official uniform was standing at our door, waiting for someone to let him in.

And that's when I knew the fun was over.

CHAPTER 31

Not Quite Lying

In a complete panic, I ran to my bedroom to hide. I left the door open a crack so I could hear what the man said to Grandma Dotty when she opened the door.

"Hello, ma'am, I'm Officer Parks from the Hills Village PD."

Can you say "heart attack"? I felt like I was going to pass out. And, of course, Rafe was conveniently nowhere in sight—so I had no one to blame!

This was it. It finally happened. My brother had turned me into a juvenile delinquent.

"You don't look like a police officer," Grandma Dotty said, while I held on to the wall and tried not to fall over.

"Sorry," he said. "I meant the Parks Department, not the Police Department."

And I thought—*Why doesn't that make me feel any better?*

"Does Georgia Kashadoodian live here?" the man said. "I'd like to ask her a few questions."

And I thought—*Yeah, that's why.*

"I'm sorry," Grandma Dotty said. "Did you say Officer Parks? From the Parks Department?"

I heard the man take a deep breath. "Yes, ma'am. I get that a lot," he said.

Meanwhile, I was wondering how fast I could tie my sheets together and climb out the window. It wouldn't be so bad. I could live out there, on the road. Nobody would even *think* to look for me in Saskatchewan....

Or maybe not. *On the run from the law* isn't my style. (But you already knew that, didn't you?)

Still, I would have cleaned Missy Trillin's private bathroom for the rest of my life if I could have slipped out of there unseen somehow.

"Georgia, honey!" Grandma Dotty called.

So I took a deep breath. I tried to focus. And I trembled my way out to the living room.

"Hi, Georgia, I'm Officer Parks," he said.

"He's from the Parks Department," Grandma Dotty said, and I saw her trying not to laugh.

I wasn't even close to laughing. It's hard to giggle when you're trying not to panic-pee in your pants.

"Um...hi," I said. "Is this about the bubbles?"

"That's right," he said. "Do you know anything about it?"

"Well, we were making a video, and it just started...bubbling," I said.

"That much we know," he said. "But it seems like quite a coincidence, just as you were performing in the park."

"So true!" Grandma Dotty said. "It looked wonderful, don't you think?"

In case you couldn't tell, my grandma marches to the beat of her own private drummer. In a good way.

But Officer Parks wouldn't get distracted. He was staring at me as if he could pull the truth out of my brain just by using his eyes. I sure wished I knew what he was thinking.

"I was surprised when it happened," I said. Which was the truth.

But I'm not sure he believed me. All of a sudden, he looked about thirty percent meaner.

"So, you don't know who put the soap in the fountain?" he asked.

I was sweating from my armpits to my pinkie toes, and I just kept thinking—*No lying, no lying, no lying*. But I had to tell him *something*.

"The truth is…" I said. "This totally sounds like something my brother would do."

"Really?" he said, and flipped open a little pad. "What's his name?"

"Rafe Khatchadorian," I said, and even gave him the right spelling. "But the thing is, Rafe couldn't have done it. He was right there in front of us the whole time."

Officer Parks flipped his pad closed and looked annoyed.

"Excuse me, young lady, but did you see who did this or not?" he asked.

"No, sir," I said. "I didn't. I really, really didn't. I never saw anyone put any soap in any fountain."

Which was also the truth.

Officer Parks gave me one more long look that felt like it took about an hour to end. Finally, he pulled out a business card and handed it to Grandma Dotty.

"If any of you can think of anything else, let me know," he said.

Grandma Dotty took one look at his name on the card, put her hand over her mouth, and said,

"Excuse me. I think something's burning in the fridge."

Then she left the room. A second later, I heard the refrigerator open, and the slightly muffled sound of giggling.

Before I could brain-melt all the way to the ground, Officer Parks gave me one last firm look. Then he turned around and let himself out while Grandma Dotty just laughed and laughed and laughed in the kitchen.

I'm glad *someone* thought it was funny.

CHAPTER 32

Well, That Explains a Thing or Two

When Rafe got home, I cornered him, dragged him into my room, and locked the door.

"Before you say a word, let me talk," Rafe said. "I knew you wouldn't go for it if I told you ahead of time. I just had to show you how awesome it could be."

"Yeah, just as awesome as a year in the state penitentiary," I said. Then I told him all about Officer Parks from the Parks Department.

Rafe thought it was funny, too.

"Am I the only one who takes things seriously around here?" I said, trying not to yell. Mom was home now, and I didn't want her getting suspicious. "I almost got *arrested!*" I whispered.

"What you *got* was a stint on the six o'clock

news," Rafe said. "Besides, we used the eco-friendly stuff. That fountain's never been cleaner."

"THAT'S NOT THE POINT!" I yelled before I could help it.

"Everything okay in there?" Mom called out.

"Fine!" I said.

When I looked back, Rafe was hooking Flip's camera up to my laptop.

"What are you doing?" I said.

"Don't you want to see the video?"

I'd totally forgotten. But now I *totally* wanted to see it.

At first, it was just us playing. We looked great in our new outfits, but otherwise there wasn't much to see. Right up until I noticed Flip lurking around the back of the fountain.

"We won't use this part, obviously," Rafe said nervously.

Uh-oh.

I saw Flip taking off his backpack. He unzipped the top, set it on the edge of the fountain, and sat down right on top of it.

That's when about a gallon of blue goopy liquid poured out.

"Wow, he must *really* like Mari," I said.

"Flip's totally crazy, in the good way," Rafe said. "He wants you guys to rock this movie more than I do, and I'm the director!"

It was like a train wreck. I couldn't tear my eyes away. I watched the whole thing straight through.

"Is this all loaded on my laptop?" I asked.

"It is now," Rafe said.

"Good," I said. Then I pressed the Erase All button on the GoBro dropdown menu and unplugged the camera.

"What are you doing?" he said. "I still have to edit that video!"

"You can do it on my computer," I said. "I'm not taking any chances."

"What makes you think it's any safer with you?" Rafe asked.

"Hmmm, let me think," I said. "There was the time you let Miller the Killer get his hands on your secret notebook."

"Well, yeah," he said, "but—"

"Then there was the time in art school when you took that kid's sculpture and it broke into a million pieces."

"That was an accident," Rafe said.

"Or the time you—"

"Okay, okay, I've got it," he said.

I probably should have just erased the whole thing from my laptop, but the rest of that video was pure gold.

Besides, I wasn't going to go to the trouble of facing down the Hills Village "PD" and nearly go to Parks Department jail, only to wind up with *nothing*. No way.

This World Tour business was turning out to be more dangerous than I thought.

CHAPTER 33

Dream On

This is the part where I'm supposed to have an awesome dream, all about how famous We Stink is going to get.

It would include talk shows and stadium dates, magazine covers, endorsements for environmentally friendly laundry detergent, and, of course, an animated We Stink movie where we save the world from evil princesses, one hit song at a time.

And the dream would just go on and on like that, until I get swallowed up by fluffy pink cotton-candy clouds of joy...

Except that's not the dream I had that night. Not even close.

Instead, I dreamed that I was on a big ship, and

Rafe was holding me by my feet while I hung off the deck over the freezing ocean. If he let go, I was going to fall straight down to a watery grave.

Plus, he kept eating handfuls of buttery popcorn from a giant bucket, and his hands were getting greasier and more slippery while he tried to hold on.

There were also a few rainbow-colored llamas and talking seagulls in there. I probably ought to lay off the Skittles before bed next time.

I'm no dream expert, but it didn't take a genius to figure out what that one meant. Some part of me was scared to death about putting my fate in Rafe's hands.

So I couldn't help looking at him a little suspiciously at breakfast. Especially because he kept grinning at me like a crazy person.

"What?" I said.

"You didn't see?"

"See what?" I was still kind of mad about the dream, even if that part wasn't technically his fault.

"You should take a look at the contest website," he said. "Because *someone* just went from forty-eighth place to—"

I didn't even hear the rest. I was already running back to my room. I threw open my laptop, clicked onto the site, and—

Forty-one.

FORTY-ONE.

FORTY-ONE!

We were in forty-first place! Overnight! I've never been so excited about such a boring number in my life.

I couldn't believe it. This was actually happening. It was all like some kind of...well...

Just like a dream.

Minus the llamas.

CHAPTER 34

Overnight Sensation

It kept going once I got to school, too. At least eight people said something nice to me on the way to my locker.

Usually, the only time I get noticed is when I take too long at the water fountain, or dork out at volleyball in gym and accidentally help the other team get a point.

"Georgia! I saw you on the news! Very cool."

"You're famous-ish!"

This was a whole new feeling. Like a bubbly, tiny-bit-famous, who's-that-oh-wait-that's-ME kind of feeling.

And I loved it.

"Hey, Georgia!" Jeanne Galletta said when she spotted me in the hall. "I heard you were on the news last night."

Not only is Jeanne really cool, she's also the editor of the online school paper, *Fine Print*. In other words, I was talking to another reporter now.

So I told her all about the band, and the contest, and our chance to warm up for Lulu and the Handbags.

"This is huge," Jeanne said.

"It is?"

"Sure. You guys are the biggest thing to happen at HVMS since...well, since your brother got arrested in the parking lot in the sixth grade." (Which is a whole other story, but we're talking about *me* right now.)

"Anyway, we totally have to do an interview with the band," Jeanne said.

"We do?" I said. "I mean, sure!"

She had already pulled out a little voice recorder and everything. "We're going to put you guys over the top," she said. "I'm going to make it my own personal mission."

It was still kind of sinking in. We Stink was *actually maybe* going to make it into the top twelve! That was a giant step up from definitely **not** going to make it, which is what I'd been thinking but just hadn't wanted to say out loud.

"So, Georgia, what's next for We Stink?" Jeanne asked, holding out the recorder.

And I gave her the only answer I knew.

"Everything!"

HVMS'S FINE PRINT

Hometown Band Bubbles to the Top!

Movie in the works!

Here's what YOU can do for We Stink!

Up next: EVERYTHING.

VOTE FOR WE STINK
CLICK HERE!

CHAPTER 35

Greatest Hits

♪ *Shake it, shake it!* ♪

Okay, everyone—turn up your speakers and cue the music!

This is the part where you see a bunch of quick movie scenes, one after the other, showing how We Stink really *was* bubbling to the top.

All of a sudden, we were everywhere.

♡ ⬭
37 likes
@WeStinkBand: We're in thirty-fifth place! Keep those votes coming! #LuluContest #VoteForWeStink #itsgonnahappen

added a new photo
Check the new look! And #VoteForWeStink!!!!!!!!!!!
VOTE FOR WE STINK
VOTE FOR WE STINK

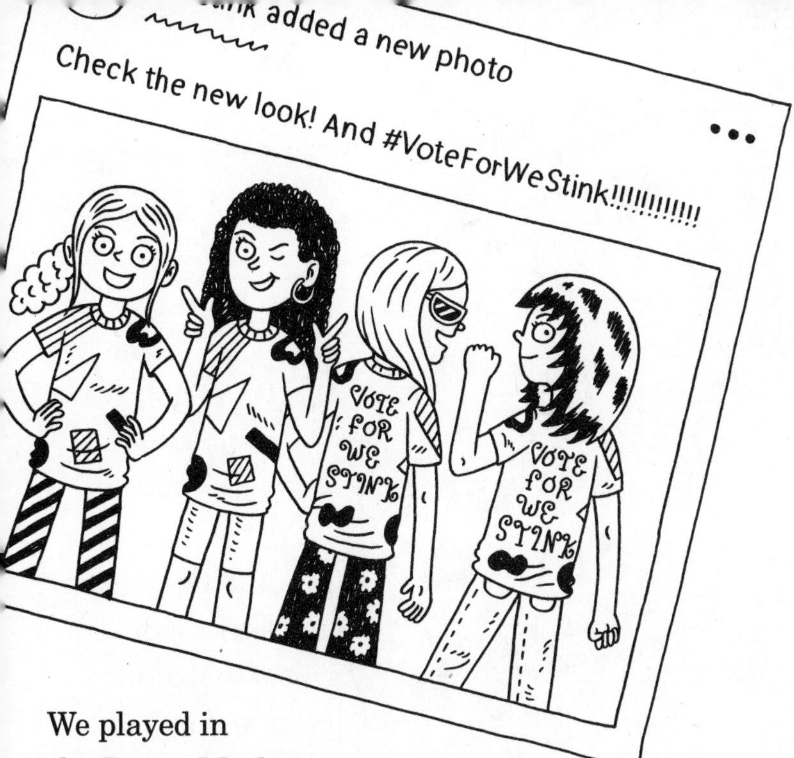

We played in
the Duper Market
parking lot that Saturday morning.
Then we swung by the public access TV studios and went on *Hills Village This Week with Marty Gruber.*

We played at a pep rally at HVMS. We also played at the elementary school, *and* the high school, *and* the senior center.

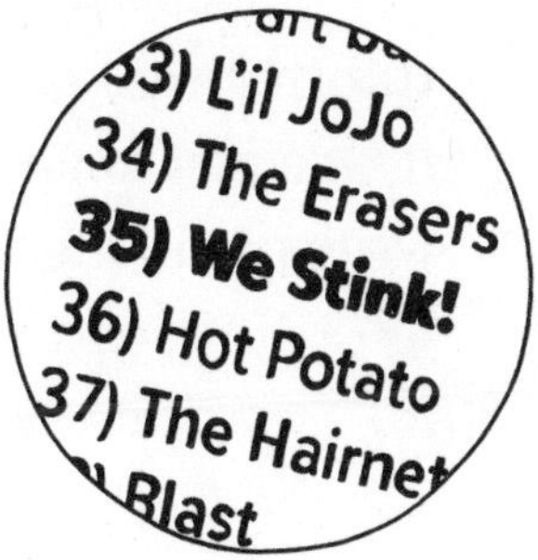

33) L’il JoJo
34) The Erasers
35) We Stink!
36) Hot Potato
37) The Hairnet
Blast

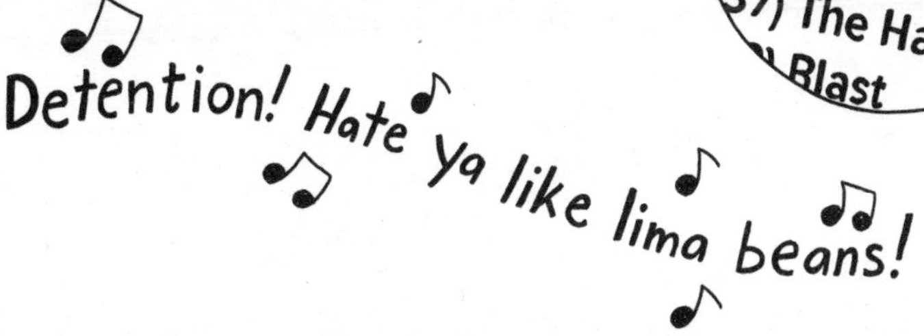

Detention! Hate ya like lima beans!

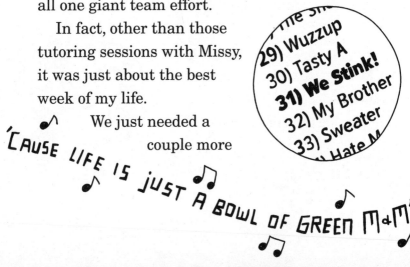

Stink added a new photo

Check us out on #hillsvillagethisweek with @MartyGruber! See your local listings for times!

That's like every age there is! Mom made us some awesome T-shirts, too. And Grandma Dotty made meatballs, lots and lots of meatballs, to get us through those long practice sessions in the garage—I mean, in We Stink Studios. And Rafe filmed the WHOLE thing. It was all one giant team effort.

In fact, other than those tutoring sessions with Missy, it was just about the best week of my life.

We just needed a couple more

29) Wuzzup
30) Tasty A
31) **We Stink!**
32) My Brother
33) Sweater
Hate M

'CAUSE LIFE IS JUST A BOWL OF GREEN M&M'S

The one thing I don't need to keep is you! ♪

events now, or even one really big one, to put us over the top. Because by the end of the week, we'd gotten all the way up to seventeenth place.

Only five more places to go, and we were headed to Lulu-Land!

Plus…I haven't even told you one of the best parts yet.

WeStinkBand

♡ ○
42 likes
@WeStinkBand: OMG, everyone…17th place!!!! Keep those votes coming! #omg #itsreallyhappening #keepthosevotescoming #VoteForWeStink

A...Plus

On top of everything else, Sam and I got an A on our Rube Goldberg machine that Friday!

The golf ball rolled down the train track and knocked the marble, and the marble went down the funnel and dropped right onto the Return button on my laptop.

It was like the cherry on top of the sundae. And in fact, I was about to get a cherry on top of the cherry, if you can believe that.

It happened when Sam and I were walking to lunch after science. I guess I was feeling extra sunshine-y good about everything. Maybe that's how I got the nerve to just go for it, once and for all.

"Can I ask you a question?" I said.

"Sure," he said.

"Don't think I'm weird, but...do you like me? And I don't just mean as a friend."

Sam looked at me like I wasn't making any sense.

"What are you talking about?" he said.

"Well, I said I liked *you* that day when you asked to be science partners. And then you didn't say anything back," I told him.

"Yes, I did," he said.

"Uh, no," I said. "You really didn't."

Sam looked at me again, but in a different way this time. He was turning red. Like, apple-red. Then he looked at the floor.

"I really stink at this," he said. "Now I feel stupid."

Which made me feel bad.

"It's okay if you don't like me, too," I said.

"No," he said, "it's not that. It's more like...well...I kind of thought you were already my girlfriend."

Believe me, that was *not* what I expected him to say. I would have been less surprised if he'd said, "I'm the reincarnation of your goldfish Squashy who you ate when you were three. Thanks for nothing."

"Wait. *What?*" I said.

"I'm so embarrassed," he said, even though now I was the one turning red.

"So, are you…are we…boyfriend and girlfriend?" I asked, still not sure about, well, *anything*.

Sam shrugged. "Do you not want to be?"

"No!" I said. "I mean—YES! I do. Want to. Be… you know."

And then some even crazier part of me took over. I can't even explain it, but I leaned in, and I kissed Sam right there on the stairs.

If I had thought about it, I probably would have remembered that we were…oh, I don't know…AT SCHOOL. Also that Mrs. Stricker has a habit of showing up out of nowhere.

Like, for instance, at that very moment.

You would have thought we were running around naked from the way she started yelling about it, too.

"EXCUSE ME! WHAT IS GOING ON HERE?"
she hollered.

Which is basically like Mrs. Stricker's favorite
song, if she had one.

"No public displays of affection are allowed in
school!" she said. "Let's go, you two—march!"

And just like that, I was in trouble again. Except this time, I didn't even care. Not one little bit. And I don't think Sam did, either.

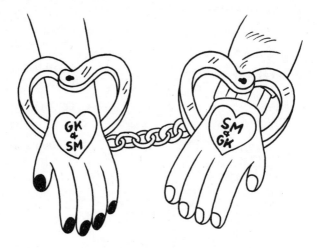

SAMSAMSAM

I barely had any time to freak out about how crazy it was that I, Georgia Khatchadorian, had a boyfriend. *My boyfriend.* That was always something other people could say, not me.

Except now—YES, ME. It was SO STRANGE. I had NO WORDS.

Actually, that's not true. I had a lot of words going through my head, but most of them were "Sam," "Sam," and "Sam."

Did I know what to do next, or how the whole girlfriend-boyfriend thing was supposed to work? Well, no. Not exactly. But then again, neither did Sam. Also known as MY BOYFRIEND.

SAM.

SAM.

SAM!

(Sigh. I was *really* happy. Can you tell?)

But like I said, I didn't get to enjoy all that for very long before a major case of trouble reared its head again.

Or maybe I should say *her* head.

You notice how short this chapter is? Well that's about how long it took for Missy Trillin to make her next move. And this one was going to be a doozy.

Turning Tables

It happened in the middle of our next tutoring session, just after I tried to show Missy how to calculate the area of a right triangle.

"So," I said, "you need to divide ab by...?"

"Eighty-four?" Missy said.

I tried not to smack my forehead.

"Two," I said.

"Whatever," she said.

I knew Missy was smarter than this. I mean, she knew all seventy-five flavors of Lip Bomb Lip Balm by heart. And we only had to know eight formulas for the quiz.

She just wasn't trying. And I wasn't sure why.

"I need a bathroom break," I said.

"Not in *my* bathroom," she said, and pointed at the door. Which was fine with me. Really, I just needed a Missy break.

So I hiked all the way down to the powder room on the first floor and took my time.

When I got back, Missy was pointing and laughing at something on her desktop computer. Then she looked at me and laughed even harder.

I looked over at the window seat, and my laptop wasn't where I'd left it. It was sitting open on the floor. And that's when I started getting scared.

"What is that?" I asked.

"I think you know," she said.

I looked closer. Right there on her screen, plain as day, I could see Flip pouring laundry detergent into Millennium Fountain all over again.

I immediately panicked.

She had evidence! She had the proof! "That's stealing!" I said, picking up my laptop.

"And *that's* vandalism," Missy said, pointing at the screen again.

"How'd you—" I said, but I was pretty sure I knew.

"Every time you go to the bathroom, I check your laptop. And guess what? I just found a gold mine," Missy said. "Ha! Ha! Ha-ha-ha-ha-ha!"

"You're not even laughing. You're just saying 'ha.'"

"Like that's the point," she said. "Now listen to me very carefully. You're going to sit next to me in that math quiz. And you're going to make sure I can see every last one of your answers. Otherwise, this little home movie of yours is going straight to the police."

"I can't do that!" I said. "That's cheating!"

"Oh, right, because you're so above cheating," she said, and pointed at the screen again. "I don't think so."

Missy was like a supervillain. No, not even. She was like the person who trains all the supervillains and makes them cry and beg for mercy before she builds them back up again. Like a criminal mastermind. She was that evil.

Or that good, depending on how you looked at it.

I knew I couldn't do this. I couldn't knowingly let Missy cheat off me, because that would make me as bad as her. But I also couldn't imagine

throwing away everything we'd worked so hard for. And the test was only three days away.

That gave me seventy-two hours to do something about this.

But *what?*

CHAPTER 39

Band Aid

I couldn't concentrate at band practice. My head was everywhere *but* in the studio, and it felt like I was trying to play my guitar with two big mittens on my hands.

I had Missy on the brain.

"Let's try that again," Nanci said. "And Georgia, pay attention. We need to get this right."

"Oh, and by the way," Mari said, "we still need to come up with a couple more events to get votes. We're so close, you guys! We can't blow it now."

"Actually," I said, "I need to tell you all something."

I couldn't stand it anymore. This was going to

explode in my face, and they'd never forgive me if it did.

So I put my guitar down and took a deep breath.

Then I told them all about what had happened. We'd never talked about who put the bubbles in the fountain, so I started at the beginning, and explained how it was Rafe's idea and how Flip had been the one with the soap.

Then I told them about Missy—every last detail.

"I'm really sorry," I said. "I was trying to keep you all out of it, but I guess I can't."

"Um...*duh?*" Patti said. "Of course Flip did it."

"You all knew?" I asked.

They all nodded.

"Well, I'm still really sorry," I said.

"It's not your fault," Nanci said.

"It kind of is," I said. "I should have just erased the video. And I should have been more careful with Missy."

"It's impossible to be careful with witches," Patti said.

"And you know what else?" Mari said. "You need to stop trying to do everything. No offense, Georgia, but you're not in charge. We're in this together."

"I know," I said. I was blushing, and my eyes were getting kind of stingy and wet. These girls were the best.

"Thanks, you guys," I said. "But what can I...I mean, what can *we* do about this?"

"Well, Rafe was the big idea guy in the park," Patti said. "What would he do now?"

"I don't want to get Rafe involved," I said. "That's like bringing a lit match to the dynamite party. He'd just mess it all up, all over—"

But then...oh. My. Brainstorm. A giant lightbulb went on in my head.

Thanks to Patti's question (and Rafe's trouble-making), I was getting an idea.

I didn't *have* to get Rafe involved. I just had to *think* like him. Which, to be honest, was starting to feel more and more like thinking like *me*.

"Georgia?" Nanci said, and waved a drumstick in front of my face. "Are you still there?"

"I've got it!" I said. "I mean, I don't want you to think I'm taking charge or anything, but I know what we have to do now. And I need all of your help to get it done."

Infiltration Station

BUZZZZZZZ!

I stepped back from the buzzer at the Trillins' gate, shushed the girls, and waited for someone to answer.

"Alloo?" a voice said. It was Nicole, the Trillins' French cook. I knew Mrs. Trillin had aquarobic yoga at her gym on Tuesday afternoons, so the timing was perfect.

"Hi, it's Georgia Khatchadorian," I said.

"Oui-oui," she said, "Come *een,* Georgia! You are here for the tutoring?"

"I'm here, all right," I said.

And the gate swung open.

Then the girls and I swung into action. We headed up the driveway but cut around the big oak tree, under the arbor on the side of the house, around the long way, and back toward the pool, where we had a perfect view of Missy's bedroom window up above.

I waved at the gardener. He was used to seeing me around, too. But still, we had to work fast. So the second we were all set up with our instruments, Nanci counted us off.

"One, two, one-two-three-four!"

We started with "Green M&M's." It didn't really matter which song we started with, as long as it was loud.

Pretty soon, Nicole came out from the kitchen.

"What *ees zis?*" she yelled.

"It's okay!" I shouted back to her. "Missy asked for it!"

Which technically, again, was true. She did ask for it!

We didn't even get to the second verse before Missy's window slammed open up above.

"WHAT DO YOU THINK YOU'RE DOING?" she screamed at us.

"CAN'T HEAR YOU!" Patti yelled.

"I SAID...*WHAT*...ARE...YOU...*DOING?*" We just ignored her and kept right on playing.

And setting the trap.

CHAPTER 41

Turning Tables, Part 2

If there's one thing Missy Trillin hates, it's being ignored. I knew she'd want to come down and personally kick us out. I was counting on it, anyway.

I also knew the house well enough to know that she'd use the back stairs and come out through the family room.

So as soon as she closed her window, I left the girls to keep playing and went in through the kitchen.

Nicole looked completely confused by now.

"Is Missy upstairs?" I asked, even though I knew the answer.

"I believe zo," Nicole said, and I kept moving. I went down the first-floor hall, up the main stairs,

back down the second-floor hall, and then *very carefully* into Missy's deserted room.

I could already hear her outside, yelling at the girls. It wasn't going to be long before she figured out what was up. I had to work ultrafast.

So I threw myself at Missy's computer. Luckily, I knew exactly what to look for. And I'd watched her log on enough to figure out her password, too.

Still, the clock was ticking. Missy had already stopped shouting, which meant she was on her way back. I could practically hear that *Mission: Impossible* theme song in my head.

My fingers flew over the keyboard. I opened a search window and looked for anything with "STINK" in it.

That did the trick. There was the video, right there. I didn't even have to open it.

Right click!

Move to Trash!

And—SLAM!

"WHAT ARE YOU DOING IN HERE???!!!"

I turned around and Missy was standing there, sweating all over the fluffy white carpet, with a *Kill-Georgia* look in her eyes.

"What do you think I'm doing?" I said. "It's already done."

Except then I realized—it wasn't. I still had to empty the trash on her computer, or she could just get the video back again.

I turned back to the mouse while Missy charged.

Right click!

Empty Trash!

She got there a microsecond too late. That file was gone, gone, gone—and just in time.

"I'm calling the police!" she said. "You just stole my property!"

"Wrong," I said. "I erased the property YOU stole from me!"

"So what?" she said. "You can't prove it."

"You also tried to blackmail me into helping you cheat," I said.

"Yeah, and I'm warning you right now," she said. "You'd better give the answers on that quiz if you know what's good for you. I can make your life very difficult if I want to."

"Actually," I said, "I don't think you will."

"Watch me," she threatened.

"Oh, I am," I told her. "And so is that little camera right there."

I pointed at the GoBro I'd left running on the desk. The one that was pointed her way and capturing the whole conversation.

"Those cameras are tiny, but they get great sound quality," I said.

"Give me that!" she said, and dove for it.

But I was one step ahead. I may limp a little when I walk, but I knew exactly what I was doing. I jumped up from the desk, grabbed the camera, ran to the window, and threw it open.

"Nanci!" I said. "Right here!"

Then I tossed the camera down to her. Nanci plays Little League *and* drums. She's got good hands. That's why we made her the catcher.

And she snagged my toss, no problem.

Missy was practically hyperventilating by now.

"Don't worry," I said. "Your secret's safe with me. I'll even help you finish studying for that quiz, if you want. But there *is* going to be one more tiny thing."

Missy looked like she wanted to explode. But we weren't quite done yet, and she knew it.

"What do you want now?" she asked.

CHAPTER 42

You're Invited

WE STINK

Is Throwing A Party—AND YOU'RE INVITED!

Come one, come all, to a fabulous pool party, concert, and video launch for WE STINK, at the even-more-fabulous Trillin Estate! Free Food, Music, Games, Prizes! And, of course, a Voting Booth where you can help put us over the top and send us to the live auditions. **AND DID WE MENTION THE FREE FOOD???** Bring your suits, your appetites, and your internet-enabled devices. We Stink will play all our greatest hits by the pool. It's gonna be **a-maaaaa-zing!**

Parrr-tay!

That Saturday, we had our Pizza-Pool-Party-Palooza for We Stink at Missy's mansion. Everyone at school knew that invitations to the Trillin estate were about as common as Willy Wonka's Golden Tickets, so we had a HUGE crowd.

Even Missy was in a good mood...for Missy. She'd gotten a B-plus on her math test, thanks to our extra tutoring sessions, and that meant she was finally reunited with her boyfriend—I mean, her phone.

Her reunion with it was kind of like watching a cheesy romance movie, except that it was with, you know, a *phone*.

It's not like Missy and I were friends now. Or even frenemies. But at least we had a truce, and that's all I needed. Because the party was capital-A-plus AWESOME.

Sam, Flip, and Jeanne all helped out. Each one of them set up a voting table for us in a different spot—by the Trillins' front gate, by the food table, and in front of the pool house.

So in other words, if you wanted to get into the party, you had to vote. If you wanted to eat, you had to vote. If you wanted to swim, you had to vote. That part was Sam's idea, and it was genius.

Meanwhile, We Stink played all our greatest hits by the pool. It was like a college party on spring break, but without any of the R-rated behavior. Unless the R stands for Rafe.

After our first set, I heard him shouting from somewhere over my head.

"Hey, everyone, up here!"

I looked up and he was on the roof of the pool house, pointing his camera down at the crowd.

"Everyone say 'We Stink!'" Rafe yelled.

"We Stink!" a bunch of people yelled.

Rafe yelled back. "I can't hear you!"

"WE STINK!" everyone yelled.

"One more time!"

"WE STINK!"

Part of me wanted to yell at him to come down and stop embarrassing me. But on the other hand, I know an amazing movie moment when I see one.

The music was jamming. Everyone was having a great time. Rafe was catching it all on camera. And the votes were pouring in.

In other words, We Stink was officially ready for takeoff!

Down to the Wire

By the end of the party, we'd gotten all the way to fourteenth place. Only two more spots to go before we made it into the live finals! But the voting was closing at midnight that night.

This was going to be a squeaker.

As soon as I got home, I went to my room, closed the door, and started checking the contest results every couple of minutes. Or more like every couple of seconds.

I also opened up a group chat with Mari, Patti, and Nanci.

PATTI: What place are we in now?

MARI: Can't you see?

PATTI: I'm too nervous to look! My eyes are shut!

NANCI: Huh?? But then how can you...never mind.

GEORGIA: Still in fourteenth place.

For a long time, nothing changed. We just stayed right there in fourteenth place while I refreshed and refreshed and refreshed that page until my thumb was ready to fall off.

But just after eleven thirty, something amazing happened. We jumped two spots, right into twelfth place.

MARI: Did you see that???

PATTI: See what?

GEORGIA: 12!!!!!!!!!!!

PATTI: IS THIS A DREAM???

NANCI: It can't be. None of us are asleep!!

MARI: I'm delirious.

NANCI: Hi, delirious, I'm Nanci.

PATTI: How much time left??

GEORGIA: Twenty-three minu—

I didn't even get to finish typing before we moved again—down to thirteenth place.

MARI: NOOOO!

PATTI: Now it's a NIGHTMARE.

But then we popped back up to twelfth.

NANCI: YESSSSSSSSSS!!!!!!

PATTI: I can't take much more of this!

MARI: How much longer now?

GEORGIA: Twenty-two and a half minutes.

Those next twenty-two and a half minutes
felt more like years. I think I grew my first gray
hairs, just watching We Stink flip from twelfth, to
thirteenth, to twelfth, to thirteenth.

And then, with only ninety seconds to go, we
double-jumped—into eleventh place.

GEORGIA: YOU GUYS!!!!

NANCI: I'm gonna pass out!

MARI: I'm gonna pee my PJs.

PATTI: I'm gonna do both!

MARI: Almost there!!!

NANCI: But not yet!

MARI: BUT ALMOST!!!!!!!

Finally, it came down to the last seconds: ten, nine, eight, seven, six, five, four, three, two, one...
The clock on my computer clicked over to midnight....
I hit Refresh one last time....
And that's when I screamed.

MARI: ELEVENTH?

NANCI: ELEVENTH!!!!

PATTI: ELEVENTH!?!?!?!?!?!?!?!?!?

GEORGIA: ELEVENTH!!!!!!!

MARI: :-)))))))))))))))))

The door to my room flew open, and Mom, Grandma, and Rafe all piled in. Grandma Dotty had a meat tenderizer held up like a weapon and Rafe had his camera. (So I guess I know who is going to save me from the murderers when they come and who is just going to put it in a movie.)

"What's wrong?" Mom said.

"NOTHING!" I screamed.

"But..."

"Eleventh place?!" Rafe said, looking at my laptop. Even he was excited. We might have even hugged or something.

Yeah, right.

"We're going to the live finals! And I'm going to meet Lulu and the Handbags!" I yelled, hopping up and down.

"I love a good handbag!" Grandma Dotty said.

Nobody was even mad about me waking them up. In fact, we broke out the leftover party food and had a pizza toast right there, in the middle of the night.

I hoped the downstairs neighbors didn't mind. Because none of us was going back to sleep anytime soon.

CHAPTER 45

Four Steps Forward, One Step Back

The next bunch of days went by in a blur of almost-famousness. We practiced whenever we could, shopped for new (used) clothes, and even did lots of interviews. By which I mean that Jeanne Galletta interviewed us three times.

Anything we could do to spread the word would only help us later. And Rafe said it all made pretty good B-roll for our Rock-You-Mentary. I guess he's right about some things.

Rarely.

I also wrote like crazy, trying out every new song idea I could think of.

NUT-FREE TABLE

Party over here at the NUT-FREE TABLE!
Party over here at the NUT-FREE TABLE!
If you get there first, please save a seat for me,
I'll bring along my sandwich, just some "J" with no "PB"
The only rule's about the nuts, don't bring them,
  none at all,
Unless you want your friend to swell up like a
  basketball.
So grab your grub and join us at our table for some
  fun.
There's always room for one more butt — a seat for
  anyone!
It doesn't matter if you're cool or smart or
  geeky or disabled,
'Cause everybody's welcome at the NUT-FREE TABLE!

By Thursday, I was ready to explode. I couldn't wait for the finals on Saturday....

And then Friday happened.

When I got to school that morning, I noticed a familiar official-looking car parked out front. And when I walked past the office, I saw a familiar face in the hall.

It was Officer Parks from the Parks Department.

Oh. My.

Unexpected twist.

I thought he was done with his "suds mountain" investigation. But maybe not.

"Good morning, Miss...Kashadooshian," he said, looking at that little detective's pad of his.

"Khatchadorian," I told him.

"That's what I meant," he said, and scribbled something down.

"Are you here about the...bubbles?" I asked him. "I thought that was all finished."

"Just because you haven't seen me doesn't mean I haven't kept busy," he said. Then he smiled at me, the same way a cobra might smile at an extra-chubby mouse.

So I got out of there while I still could. But

something told me we weren't done with the nasty surprises that morning.

And we weren't. In the middle of first period, Mrs. Stricker got on the PA system.

"Excuse the interruption," she said. "Flip Savage, please report to the office."

It's not like she said, "Flip Savage, please report to the office for interrogation and arrest." But she didn't have to. As soon as I heard Flip's name, I knew exactly what was going on.

FACT: Flip was the one who poured that soap into the fountain at City Hall Park.

FACT: The only people who knew about it were Flip, Rafe, We Stink, and one other person. One extra-mean, strawberry-scented, fashion-plated T. rex of a human being, with the initials M.T.

FACT: My truce with Missy Trillin had just expired like a month-old bottle of milk.

FACT: I had to do something about this. *Right now.*

CHAPTER 46

Damage Control

I couldn't let Flip just hang in the wind. He only put that soap in the fountain for the sake of *our* video. The right thing to do was march down to the office and turn myself in, ASAP.

But not before I dealt with Missy.

"Mr. Burdick?" I asked, raising my hand. "Can I go to the bathroom?"

"You can wait," he said. "The period's almost over."

Normally, I would have been a good girl and left it at that. Except I didn't have time for *good*. I needed to be just a little bit bad.

"Mr. Burdick?" I said.

"What now, Georgia?" he asked.

"I don't feel so well," I said. I put my hand over my mouth and puffed out my cheeks. "I think the eggs I had for breakfast weren't so fresh."

"Do you need a bucket?!" he asked, looking around. Cara Snow grabbed the trash can.

"I think I can...get to the bathroom," I said, and made a few little pukey sounds for good measure.

"Just go!" Mr. Burdick said. So I went.

I didn't go to the bathroom, though. I went straight to my locker, pulled out my laptop, and sat down right there in the hall.

Missy wasn't the only one with a dangerous secret. I still had that recording from when she tried to blackmail me into cheating. I also had her mom's e-mail address from my prison sentence days. So I fired off a quick message.

Dear Mrs. Trillin,

I hate to be the cause of any trouble, but my conscience won't let this rest. I am attaching the recording of a conversation I had with Missy before last week's math quiz. I think it speaks for itself.

Sincerely,

Georgia Khatchadorian

P.S. Thank you again SO much for the pool party!

As soon as I clicked Send I was on the move again. I knew Missy had computer lab first period, and I wanted to tell her about this, face to lying two-face.

"Excuse me, Mrs. Longine?" I asked when I got to the lab. "I'm supposed to bring Missy Trillin to the office."

Missy looked at me like I was a bad smell that had just floated into the room. She knew I was lying, but I could tell she was curious.

"What's this about?" Mrs. Longine asked.

"I don't know. Mrs. Stricker just said we should come right away," I told her, and then waited in the hall.

As soon as Missy came out, I pounced.

"I thought we had a deal," I said.

"Are you obsessed with me or something?" Missy said. "I don't know what you're talking about."

"You know as well as I do why Flip Savage got called to the office," I told her.

Missy scoffed and flipped her hair in my face. "I don't care *who* gets called to the office, as long as it's not me," she said.

"Don't bother playing dumb," I said. "I just wanted to let you know that your mom's going to be getting a certain message from me anytime now."

"Excuse me?" she said.

At that exact moment, Missy's precious phone dinged. She looked down at it, and there was a new text waiting for her. Probably from her mom.

"WHAT DID YOU DO?" Missy said.

"Let's just say you probably won't be burning through your data plan anytime soon," I told her.

Then I took off for the office. It would have been fun to stick around and watch Missy self-destruct, but I didn't have the time. I still had to save Flip.

Or, as my brother might say—this mission wasn't over yet.

CHAPTER 47

And the Surprises Just Keep on Coming. Not in a Good Way.

I was almost to the office door when someone grabbed me, pulled me back, and dragged me around the corner.

It was Rafe.

"Where have you been?" he said.

"Let go!" I said. "I have to get to—"

"The office, yeah, I know," he said. "But I came here to stop you."

"What is this, a Terminator movie?" I said. "Flip needs our help!"

"Just listen!" Rafe said. He checked over his

shoulder and then went on in a whisper. "Flip is the one who tipped off that Parks Department guy."

"*What?*" I said "Why?"

"We got it all figured out," Rafe said. "Officer Parks came to the house again last week asking even more questions. I didn't tell you because I knew you'd flip out. Flip's going to take one for the team. And you four are going to chip in ten bucks an hour for whatever they make him do."

This was all moving too fast, even for me.

"But...he could get in big trouble," I said.

"Nah. They'll just make him pick up trash in the park for a couple of hours," Rafe said. "It'll be like five bucks each."

If this were about anything besides punishments, I would have thought my brother didn't know what he was talking about. But he's pretty much an expert in that department.

And besides, Flip wasn't the problem anymore. Not even close. Because I'd just picked a major fight with Missy for no good reason.

In other words, I'd just reactivated the meanest girl in Hills Village, along with her army of spies and unlimited resources. Missy wasn't going to stop now until the Princess Patrol hunted me down, dead or alive.

I wasn't even sure which sounded worse.

Lying Low in High Places

I didn't tell Rafe a thing. It was too risky.

I couldn't tell the girls, either. Not on the day before the Lulu finals. And not after everything I'd already put them through.

The only person I *could* talk to was Sam. So I dropped a note in his locker and told him where to find me. Then I did something that I've never done before.

I skipped class.

If I wanted to avoid seeing Missy, then I had to avoid being seen, period. Her spies were everywhere.

I ducked out the nearest side door and hid behind the gym until Sam came to find me. While I waited, I tried to think of a way to undo my own stupidity.

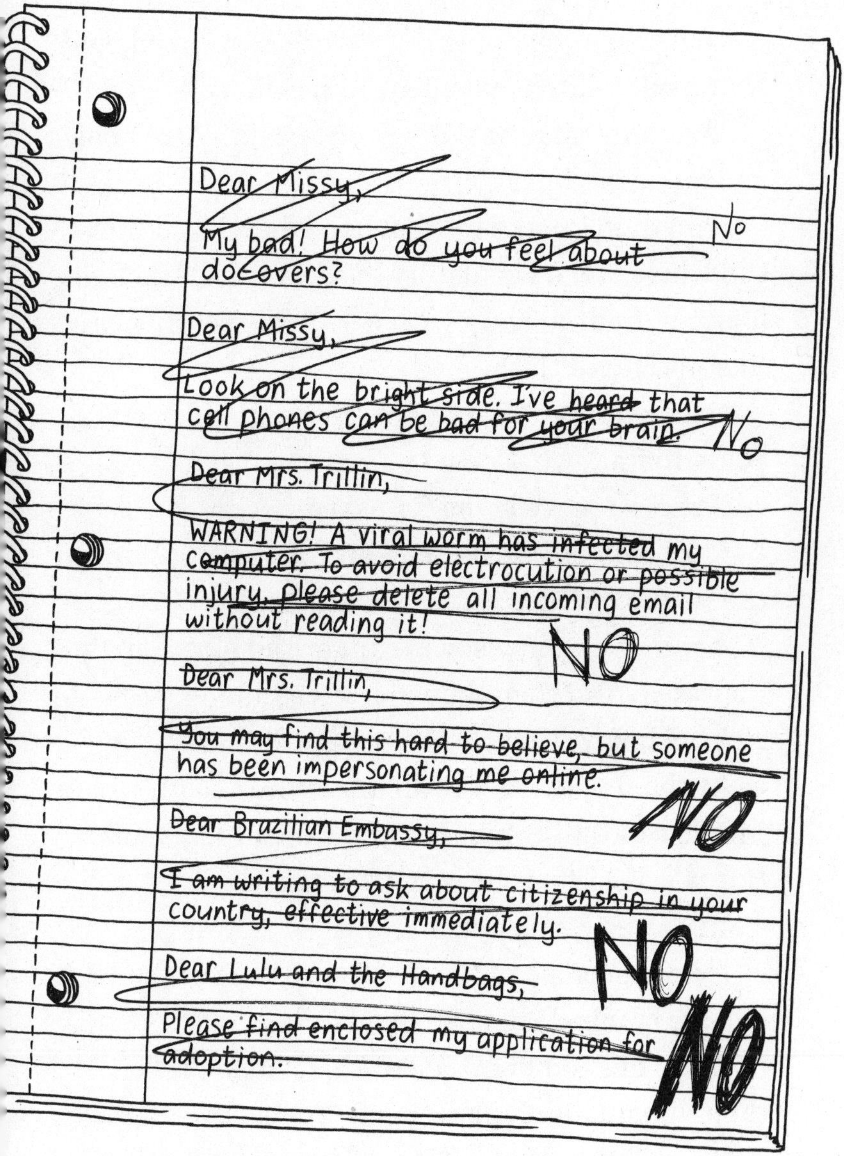

Dear Missy,

My bad! How do you feel about do-overs? No

Dear Missy,

Look on the bright side. I've heard that cell phones can be bad for your brain. No

Dear Mrs. Trillin,

WARNING! A viral worm has infected my computer. To avoid electrocution or possible injury, please delete all incoming email without reading it! NO

Dear Mrs. Trillin,

You may find this hard to believe, but someone has been impersonating me online. NO

Dear Brazilian Embassy,

I am writing to ask about citizenship in your country, effective immediately. NO

Dear Lulu and the Handbags,

Please find enclosed my application for adoption. NO

193

"What are you doing out here?" Sam asked, and I jumped. I didn't even hear him coming.

"Avoiding a natural disaster," I said. "Also known as Hurricane Missy."

Sam didn't make me feel bad when I told him the whole story. He just listened carefully, thought about it, and came up with a sensible solution. Just like in science class.

"Well, you can't stay here," he said. "Someone's going to find you. Come on."

"Where are we going?" I asked.

"I know a place," he said, and we took off toward the playing fields.

A minute later, we were under the bleachers by the track. And then Sam started climbing, with me right behind.

At the top, there was an announcer booth where people ran the scoreboard and called the games. But it was locked the rest of the time.

"In here," Sam said.

He pushed one of the floorboards out of the way, and we climbed right up inside.

"How did you know about this?" I asked. "I thought you didn't play sports."

"I don't," he said. "I'm the track and field statistician."

"Oh," I said. That made more sense.

"Also, you're not the only one who ever had to get away from bullies," he said.

I felt like little hearts were shooting right out of my eyes and bouncing off of Sam's cute face. This wasn't exactly a romantic moment, but he *was* killing it in the boyfriend department.

"So, what do I do about Missy?" I asked.

"Nothing for now," Sam said. "You need to focus on We Stink until the live finals are over."

We decided I'd stay out of sight until the end of the school day. Saturday was the finals, and we were leaving for the city at the crack of dawn. Then on Sunday I'd explain everything to Mom and beg for forgiveness. I'd probably still get in some trouble, but right now I had to prioritize.

1. The live finals
2. Everything else

So that was the plan. I'd worry about Missy after the weekend. I mean, unless We Stink won the whole competition, got instantly famous, went out on tour, and never had to come back to Hills Village ever again.

Because, hey, you never know.

Road Tripping

It wasn't easy, but I made it all the way to the next morning without a full-scale Missy Trillin attack.

At 6:00 a.m., we piled into two vans and took off for the big city. Mom, Rafe, and Grandma Dotty took the equipment in our car, and I went with the girls and Nanci's dad in their van.

Still, I didn't breathe a sigh of relief until I saw the THANKS FOR VISITING HILLS VILLAGE sign on the edge of town. In fact, I don't think I breathed at all.

"You're awfully quiet," Patti said. "What's wrong?"

"I'm just nervous," I said.

"Who isn't?" Mari said. "Maybe we should practice."

The song we'd picked for the finals was "Let's Shake on It," but with a new arrangement. This was the biggest thing any of us had ever done, so we decided it was only fair to split up the lead vocals.

"What's my first line again?" Patti asked.

"'I'm your girl, watch me twirl,'" I told her.

"No, that's *your* line," Mari said. "Patti's line is 'You're my guy, I'll watch you fly.'"

"Oh gosh, what if we forget?" Patti said.

"Maybe we should have practiced more," I said.

"You guys! We'll be fine!" Nanci said. "Just remember to come in together on the chorus."

We'd worked out some cool harmony for that part, too, and tried it again in the car.

"Let's shake on it!" we sang. "Shake-a-shake-a-shake-a-shake, let's shake on it!"

"Okay, *that* sounded amazing," Nanci said. Which it actually did.

But still, I kept thinking about Missy popping out of a guitar case to strangle me. Or showing up backstage with a couple of hired hit men. Or using her Trillin money to shut down the city completely.

Between all that, and the fact this was THE BIGGEST DAY OF MY LIFE, I was shaking, all right.

Straight out of my two-dollar thrift-store super-cool rock-and-roll boots.

Welcome to the Big Time

From the second we got out of the car in front of the theater, they kept us moving.

There were people in red Lulu sweatshirts everywhere, herding kids and instruments from the street into the lobby. It wasn't exactly the red carpet, but it was incredibly exciting.

Inside, the theater itself was GI-GAN-TIC. It felt like walking into the Grand Canyon. In a cool, exciting, and completely terrifying kind of way.

Meanwhile, everywhere I looked, there was another band of kids who seemed cooler or more confident or more talented or better dressed than us.

Or all of the above. I just hoped we didn't get eaten alive by the competition.

"Georgia, how are you feeling?" Rafe asked, sticking his camera in my face.

I wanted to say, "I feel like throwing up." But this was for our Rock-You-Mentary, so I just said, "I feel awesome! Let's do this!"

Pretty soon, a voice boomed over a microphone out of nowhere.

"EXCUSE ME, EVERYONE! PLEASE TAKE YOUR SEATS. BAND MEMBERS IN THE FIRST FIFTEEN ROWS, FAMILY IN THE LAST FIFTEEN ROWS, BEHIND THE YELLOW TAPE. WE WILL BE STARTING SHORTLY, SHORTLY, VERY SHORTLY!"

It was all a blur now. Mom and Grandma Dotty hugged me and wished us luck.

"You're going to do great, honey!" Mom said. "Don't be nervous."

But I was trembling like a plate of Jell-O in an earthquake. "Everyone else looks so...*ready*," I said.

"I'll tell you a secret," Mom said. "A lot of these kids are thinking the same thing—that *everybody else* looks like they know exactly what they're doing."

"I doubt that," I said.

"Just focus on being yourselves," Mom said. "It got you this far, right?"

"Come on, Georgia, we've got to go!" Patti said.

And I decided right there that Mom was right. We'd made it into the top twelve, after all. This was our chance to do something amazing, whether or not we won the whole thing.

And who knew? Maybe…just maybe…we'd surprise them all.

Starting with ourselves.

CHAPTER 51

Here Comes the Judge

As soon as everyone was in their seats, the lights in the theater went down. A spotlight hit the stage, and some guy I'd never seen before walked into the light.

"Gooooooooood morning, Lulu fans!" he shouted into his microphone.

He was wearing a shimmery gold jacket and had a purple stripe up the middle of his hair.

"I am your head judge, Jordy Swivel," he said.

A bunch of people applauded, mostly from the parents' section.

"Thank you, thank you!" he said. "Some of you

may know me from my number one hit single, 'Angel in Neon Legwarmers.'"

"From which century?" Patti whispered.

Nanci was already looking him up on her phone and showed me a picture.

Jordy Swivel 1982

"In just a few minutes, we will move you backstage, where you'll wait to be called for your individual performances," Mr. Swivel told us. "Meanwhile, remember, you are here to make great music."

I squeezed Mari's hand. My stomach was still doing Olympic gymnastics, but at least my breakfast was staying put.

"We want to hear what YOU can do," Mr. Swivel said. "Not what someone else can do."

And I thought—wow, he sounds just like Mom.

"This is a serious competition," he went on. "And it comes with a serious prize."

That was true, too. No matter what else happened, we were going to meet Lulu and the Handbags tonight!

"So if you're not scared to death right now, you're doing something wrong," Mr. Swivel said. "Because, trust me, kids, rock and roll is a vicious business. There's always someone ready to throw you under the bus, max out your credit card, and skip town with your girlfriend in Milwaukee when you least expect it—"

A woman ran onto the stage. She had a headset and a clipboard, and she whispered something to Mr. Swivel.

"Right! Yes!" he said sheepishly. "So as I was saying, the most important thing today is to have fun! Am I right?"

We all sort of applauded. Sort of nervously.

"Then let's get this party started!" he said. "Good luck everyone, and I'll see *you* ON STAGE!"

Special Delivery

Here's another fact for you. The room where you wait backstage is called the green room, but there's nothing green about it. It was just folding chairs, bottles of water, and a lot of nervous people. They should call it the sweat lodge, if you ask me.

Every few minutes, the door would open, and the lady with the headset would call out two more names.

"Extra Creddit! Come with me! You're up next," she said this time. "Selfie Town, you're on deck!"

"How much longer?" Patti asked.

"I wish I knew," I said.

So far, four bands had gone and eight of us were

still waiting. We were supposed to sit quietly, so it was just tick, tick, tick, tick, tick on the clock, until suddenly—

"Excuse me? Are you We Stink?" someone asked.

I jumped up, but it wasn't the headset lady. It was some guy with a messenger bag and a T-shirt that said "Spee-Dee Delivery."

"Yes, we stink!" I said. "I mean, we *are* We Stink."

"This is for you," he said, and gave me a big envelope addressed to the band.

"What is it?" Mari asked.

"I don't know," I said.

I'd never gotten a special delivery before. My hands shook when I ripped open the package.

Four smaller envelopes fell out. They were a pretty shade of lavender, with our names on them in fancy calligraphy. They also all said, "Open me just before you go on! Good luck!"

"Ooh, maybe it's a present from Lulu!" Nanci said.

And I thought, *maybe it's from Sam*. That would be just like him. He was so thoughtful that way.

Then the green room door opened and the stage manager called out again.

"Selfie Town, come with me, please! We Stink, you're on deck!"

My breakfast did one more triple-twisting flip in my stomach. This was the moment we'd been waiting for.

"We'd better open these now!" Mari said, and we all tore into our envelopes at the same time.

Nanci pulled out some papers. So did Mari and Patti. But when I looked in my envelope, it was empty. There was nothing inside. Just the faint smell of strawberries.

Although, not exactly, I thought. It smelled more like...Strawberry Split Lip Bomb Lip Balm.

Missy's favorite flavor.

"Wait!" I yelled at the girls. "Don't read those!"

But it was too late. They were already looking at their papers. And not in a happy, smiley kind of way.

"You think I can't sing?" Patti said.

"You think I'm too insecure?" Mari said.

"YOU THINK I TALK TOO LOUD?" Nanci said, waving her pages in my face.

That's when I got a glimpse of what they'd been reading. It looked like pages out of my journal—but it wasn't my journal. And it looked like my handwriting—but it wasn't my handwriting.

And I knew right then that I hadn't done nearly enough to get away from Missy Trillin and her wrath. Because guess what?

Rock stars and evil princesses have one thing in common: they never take the weekend off.

CHAPTER 53

Peace, Love, and Misunderstanding

How could you do this?" Mari said.

"I didn't!" I said. "Missy did. Those are obviously fake!" With all that tutoring, she'd definitely gotten plenty of samples of my handwriting.

"If this is fake, how did Missy know I liked Kyle Berg?" Patti said, waving more pages around.

"Or about my embarrassing birthmark?" Mari whispered. "It's all here."

All of a sudden, I was thinking about our We Stink band meetings in the bathroom at school. And how we never did check the stalls. And how much I was wishing we had.

"Don't you see? This is exactly what Missy wanted!" I said. "I was going to warn you, but I didn't want you to freak out before the finals—"

"Too late for that," Mari said.

"This isn't the first time you've lied to us, Georgia," Nanci said.

"I wasn't lying!" I said. "I was just—"

"Hang on. There's more here," Mari said, still reading. Then she looked right at Patti. "You told Georgia I wasn't pulling my weight? Why would you say that?"

"I didn't!" Patti said, and then she looked right at me. "Why would you write that, Georgia?"

"I DIDN'T! AREN'T YOU LISTENING TO ME?" I said, right before the stage manager opened the green room door again.

"Okay, We Stink, you're up! Come with me, please. Lila and the Carry-Ons, you're on deck!"

I couldn't believe it. Everything had come down to this—one big, fiery ball of disaster at the exact wrong moment. The timing could not have been worse.

Somewhere, Missy Trillin was looking into her magic witch's mirror and laughing her butt off.

Shake It Up

Five horrible minutes later, we were up on stage, plugged in and waiting to go. The theater was too dark to see anyone, and my mind was running like cuh-razy.

There hadn't been a chance to say anything else, and all I could think now was that I'd told them the truth. Those pages weren't mine.

What more could I do?

"Okay, next up we have..." Mr. Swivel's voice came over a microphone. "We Stink? Interesting name. Whenever you're ready, girls."

A spotlight hit me in the eyes. I took a deep breath. And Nanci counted us off.

"One! Two! One-two-three-four!"

I tried to focus during the intro. Still, you could feel the tension all over the stage. Nobody was looking at me, and the music was...

Well, actually, the music was *thumping*. In a good way. It felt kind of angry, and loud, and really rock-and-roll-y.

I just wished the girls had believed me. I was telling the truth. Those pages weren't mine.

And I couldn't get that thought out of my head. *FOCUS, GEORGIA!*

Mari was glaring at me now, and I realized I was about to miss my cue. So I stepped up to the mic just in time and blurted out the first line.

Sort of. Because what I sang was—

"I told you the truth. Those words weren't mine!"

Oh. My. *OOPS!*

The girls all looked at me, completely stunned. Patti didn't have any time to react, either. Her line was next. But then she shocked me right back when she sang—

"Yeah right, don't try, 'cause we all think you're lyin'!"

I went with it.

"I'm telling you now, it's all just fake!" I sang, and Nanci brought it home.

"Yeah, right, you liar," she sang, and I saw her eyes get big. She knew what to do. "Just watch my head shake!"

And we all sang—

"Shake it, shake it, shake-a-shake-a-shake it, let's shake on it!"

It was like a rock-and-roll miracle. Just like that, we were right back in it. I don't think the audience even knew the song was supposed to go another way.

I'm not saying I'm glad we got into that fight, but I'll tell you something else. The madder we got, the better the music got. And for the first time in my life, I wasn't just pretending to be a rock star.

I actually felt like one.

CHAPTER 55

And the Winner Is...

All of the Hills Village people cheered like crazy when we finished. The judges just scribbled something on their pads. Mr. Swivel said, "Thank you!" into his mic, and that was it.

I felt GREAT. It was like all the drama had just been erased and we were right back on track. Whether or not we won, the girls and I had just pulled off something amazing. So I turned to Mari, held up my hand for a high five...

And she just walked away from me, right off the stage. Patti and Nanci were right behind her, leaving me standing there with my hand in the air and my face getting redder by the second.

So much for erasing all the drama, I guess.

Afterward, in the green room, it was so quiet you would have thought someone had pressed the Mute button. As far as I could tell, Mari was mad at Patti, Nanci was mad at Mari, everyone was mad at me, and nobody was talking to anyone. I didn't even know if We Stink had just broken up, or what.

Which was too bad, because we'd just played the best show of our lives.

After all the bands performed, they finally brought all of us back out onstage for the results. We stood there in a big line while Mr. Swivel got up in front of the families again.

"Well, well, well, isn't this exciting?" he said, and you could just feel all the kids onstage grinding their teeth down to little nubs, waiting to hear who had won.

I still wanted this. I wanted it so bad. Then maybe we could start to put the whole stupid fight behind us and just keep going.

"And our winner today—"

I mean, I could live with not winning if I had to. I just didn't want to have to.

"—is a band that showed the musical chops to stand toe-to-toe with the one and only Lulu and the Handbags—"

"JUST SAY IT!" someone yelled in the audience, and everyone laughed. Mr. Swivel kept going.

"As hard as this decision was, it was also unanimous," he said. "So, without further delay, the winning band is…"

I swallowed hard. It felt like choking down a rock.

No pun intended.

"Extra Creddit!"

A big spotlight came on and Extra Creddit was high-fiving and jumping around, while the rest of us stood around like a giant pile of leftovers.

And just like that…it was all over.

Truthfully, I never thought we'd get as far as we did. But once that happened, I wanted to hear Jordy Swivel say "WE STINK IS THE WINNER!" as much as I've ever wanted anything. Now, the girls and I were just standing there with nothing to say.

And I was starting to think that We Stink—one of the best things to ever happen to me—was no more.

If the Lulu show hadn't been that night, I would have asked Mom to sneak me out of the theater in a suitcase and get me home ASAP.

But no way. Not after everything else. I was going to stick around and meet Lulu, even if it killed me.

Which it practically did.

You'll see.

And Then This Happened

The concert was amazing times infinity. Lulu was everything I wanted her to be. Heck, she was everything *I* wanted to be. It didn't even seem real that I was going to actually meet her, until we were finally allowed to line up after the show.

I ran down the aisle to be first. Rafe was right there with his camera and Mom was getting the car so we could make a quick getaway after this. I just couldn't face the girls. I'd have to work it out with them later. *Somehow.*

They set Lulu up at a table on the stage, and we were supposed to come up, one by one, get an autograph, take a picture, and then maybe die of happiness.

"Okay, let's get rolling!" the stage manager said, and pointed at me. "You're up first, young lady."

And then I was climbing the stairs.

And then I was ON STAGE. WITH LULU.

AND LULU WAS TALKING TO ME.

I mean, her mouth was moving, but all I could hear was the sound of happy fireworks exploding in my brain.

"Hello?" Lulu said, and waved a hand in my face.

"Sorry!" I kind of gasped out. I felt like a horse had just sat on my lungs. But not in a bad way.

"You want me to sign that T-shirt, hon?" Lulu asked.

I gave her the shirt while time stood still.

"And now a picture," the stage manager said. "Do you have a camera?"

I'd forgotten to borrow Mom's phone, but Rafe was still there.

"I've got this," he said.

They let me come around behind the table so we could pose in front of the drums and amps and everything. And by *everything,* I mean Lulu. She was right there, touching me. And even breathing on me. It was the best moment of my life.

"Say 'rock and roll!'" Rafe said.

"Rock and roll!" Lulu said.

And—click!

"Thanks for coming," Lulu said. "Rock on, sister!"

I sort of laughed and sort of grunted. I didn't even realize I was backing up. It was like Lulu was the sun and I couldn't stay too close or I'd burst into flames.

"Thank *you*," I said. "I, uh…love your music… and…"

"Watch out!" she said.

"You, too!" I said—right before I backed into Brandy Venner's twenty-piece drum kit.

Correction: Right before I *fell* into Brandy Venner's drum kit, knocked over the snare, stumbled into the stool, fell backward onto the floor, and brought down a whole set of cymbals and woodblocks, right on top of myself.

OMG.

It all made this giant, banging, clanging car-crash sound while I hit the dirt like a piece of rock-and-roll roadkill.

I screamed.

Lulu screamed.

And that made everyone—and I mean *everyone*—stop and stare at me sprawled out with my thrift-shop skirt around my head.

And just in case you're wondering—no, it's not possible to make yourself disappear through the floor no matter *how* much you wish for it.

The stunned silence was finally broken when Rafe shouted, "Georgia!"

"You okay, sweetheart?" Lulu asked.

"I can't believe this," the stage manager said as she pulled me out of the wreckage.

"I'm fine," I muttered, pulling my skirt back down where it belonged.

"She's okay, she's okay!" Lulu was saying.

A lot of the other kids were laughing, or trying not to. Some of them clapped. And Rafe was pushing his way toward me.

"Georgia! Georgia!" he yelled again. When I looked, he had his camera pointed right at me. "What are you thinking about, right now—?"

GET THAT CAMERA OUT OF MY FACE!!

I probably don't have to tell you that I didn't stick around after that. I hit the stairs, ran up the aisle, and kept going.

The last thing I heard was Lulu, still back on the stage.

"Now that, ladies and gentlemen," she said, "is what you call rock and roll!"

CHAPTER 57

Virally Yours

Do you remember at the beginning of this book when I told you I got famous? Well, this might not have seemed like the time for that to happen, but it was.

I was literally an overnight sensation.

I didn't find out about it until noon the next day. And even then, I only woke up because Rafe was pounding on the door.

"Georgia!"

"What do you want?" I asked.

I felt like a piece of gum stuck to the sidewalk. The last thing I wanted to do was peel myself out of bed. Much less see anyone.

But Rafe barged in anyway. "Where's your computer?" he asked.

You can probably guess where this is going, right? My brother had posted his video of me falling into Lulu's drums, and let's just say that it was WAY more popular than We Stink.

By the time I found "Clumsy Girl Wrecks Lulu's Drums" on YouTube, it had a lot of views.

Clumsy Girl Wrecks Lulu's Drums
11,312 views

"I took mine down when I saw what was happening," Rafe said, "but by then, it kind of had a life of its own—"

"Just…stop talking," I told him.

Because there was more. Lots more.

I did a search for "Clumsy Girl Lulu Drums" and got back *hundreds* of results. Some of them were just copies of Rafe's video, but there was also one with meowing sounds for no good reason, a bunch of slow-motion versions, and at least two videos with a big fart noise added in when I fell.

"On the bright side, you're kind of famous," Rafe said. "I mean, eleven thousand hits—"

"GET OUT!" I hollered. And for once, my brother knew what was good for him. He left me alone after that.

I couldn't believe this was happening. And in fact, "Clumsy Girl" was just getting started. My video was like one of those snowballs rolling down a ski slope, getting bigger and bigger by the second. Because guess what?

Eleven thousand hits was *nothing*.

CHAPTER 58

Five Days Later...

In case you can't tell, I spent a lot of time in my room that week. And a lot of that time, I was writing.

I didn't know if it was poetry or songs or what. Not that I had a band to make songs with anymore. But Mom said I didn't have to know what it was, and to just keep writing what I felt.

What I *felt* like was shipping myself off to Bolivia in a Georgia-sized container. But that wasn't going to happen.

Meanwhile, the phone was ringing off the hook.

I got invited back to *Hills Village This Week with Marty Gruber*. Another TV show in the city wanted me to come in and re-create my big fall in their studio. And I heard from Carly Morehead at Channel 12, who wanted to "profile Clumsy Girl, up close and personal" for the weekend news.

No, no, no, no, no.

So, yeah, I was famous, all right. It was like I'd gotten exactly what I'd been wishing for.

Just without any of the good parts...and all of the bad.

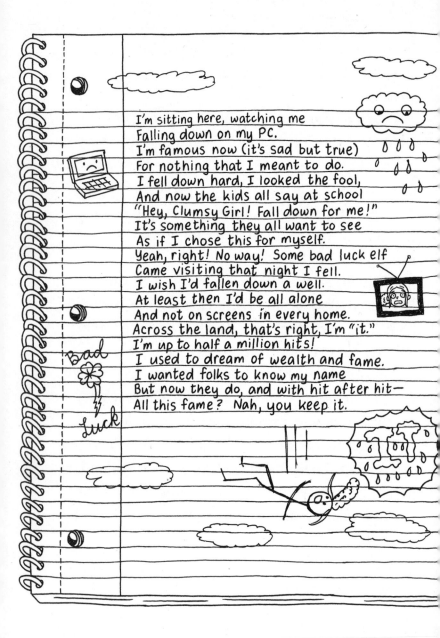

I'm sitting here, watching me
Falling down on my PC.
I'm famous now (it's sad but true)
For nothing that I meant to do.
I fell down hard, I looked the fool,
And now the kids all say at school
"Hey, Clumsy Girl! Fall down for me!"
It's something they all want to see
As if I chose this for myself.
Yeah, right! No way! Some bad luck elf
Came visiting that night I fell.
I wish I'd fallen down a well.
At least then I'd be all alone
And not on screens in every home.
Across the land, that's right, I'm "it."
I'm up to half a million hits!
I used to dream of wealth and fame.
I wanted folks to know my name
But now they do, and with hit after hit—
All this fame? Nah, you keep it.

Bad

Luck

CHAPTER 59

Sweet and Sour

After five days of the whole Clumsy Girl disaster, I felt like I had this giant We Stink–shaped hole in my life.

I missed Mari, Nanci, and Patti.

But even more than that, I missed We Stink. I missed being part of a band.

That afternoon, I went down to the studio to be alone and practice my guitar—but it didn't feel like a studio anymore. Now it was just the garage again. So I sat there, trying to play but mostly just trying not to cry.

And then I heard a familiar voice.

"How's it going in here?" Sam asked. I hadn't

even heard him come in, but I stopped playing as soon as I saw him.

"Don't stop," he said. "It sounded good. Oh, and I brought you these."

He handed me a pack of Skittles—the extra-sour kind. Those were my favorite, which was super-sweet of him. But when I tried to eat one, the giant lump in my throat got in the way.

"I don't want to cry in front of you," I said. "I'm so embarrassed. About all of it."

"It's okay if you do," he said. "I don't mind."

And even though I still didn't want to cry, I couldn't help it.

"I know I should try to focus on the positive," I said. "That's what Mom always tells me."

"That's good advice," Sam said. "But sometimes you need to be sad for a while first."

I just kind of looked at him then, with my eyes all red and puffy. I knew Sam was smart in school, but I didn't know he was smart about this stuff, too. It helped, some. I even managed to share those Skittles with him after a little while.

So it wasn't all bad.

Just *mostly* bad.

But Then...

Georgia!" Mom said, knocking on my door that night. "There's someone on the phone for you."

"Is it Sam?" I asked.

"No," Mom said.

"Then no thanks," I said.

She opened my door anyway and held out the phone. "It's from the mayor's office," she said. "I think you're going to want to take this one."

I wasn't so sure. What now? Did they want Clumsy Girl to fall off a Fourth of July parade float or something?

"Hello?" I said.

"Hi Georgia, my name is Britt and I'm calling

from the Hills Village Arts Council," she said. "I saw your video online—"

"I'm not interested," I said.

"Excuse me?" she said.

"Clumsy Girl has no comment," I said.

"Sorry. I don't know what you're talking about," the woman told me. "I'm calling about the We Stink Rock-You-Mentary, but maybe I have the wrong number."

And that's when everything started to change again.

CHAPTER 61

Not Exactly Over

So what do you want from us, Georgia?" Patti
asked.

I'd basically forced the girls to come over to the
studio. We Stink hadn't practiced in a week, and
maybe didn't exist anymore.

I didn't know how long I could keep them there,
so I got right to it.

"We've been invited to perform at City Hall," I
said.

"Again?" Mari said.

"Not in the park. Legitimately. Inside the main
auditorium," I said. "And they want to show Rafe's
movie, too."

I'd stopped calling it "our" movie. The whole time I'd been hibernating in my room, Rafe was in his room, editing that thing like a mad video scientist and getting it posted online everywhere. I knew he felt bad about what had happened, and besides, I just didn't have the energy to kill him anymore. In fact, I was actually pretty grateful for his help, despite how it all went down in the end.

"I don't know, Georgia," Nanci said. "I'll come to the movie, but I don't want to perform."

"Yeah," Patti said, and Mari nodded.

"I understand," I said.

And I did. This was my own fault. I should have trusted the girls before the finals and told them the truth right away. But *noooooo,* I had to go and turn a really good thing into a big sloppy mess instead. I tried to solve all of our problems on my own, but we were a band—a team. And now I know what happens when you try to solve things alone.

Disaster.

They'd already accepted my apology, but only in that way where it was still kind of weird and cold between all of us.

"No offense, Georgia," Patti said. "I guess maybe We Stink should just take a break for a while."

I didn't point out the obvious part. We Stink already *was* taking a break. And I've seen enough romantic comedies to know what that really meant. *Taking a break* always comes right before the saddest part of the movie.

But I didn't push it. I said I'd just meet them

at City Hall on the night of the screening. And everyone said okay, even though it seemed like we weren't even friends anymore.

But I wasn't giving up, either. If you haven't noticed yet, I don't give up. I'm a Khatchadorian.

I still had at least one more idea.

So I went back to my room, closed the door, and kept on writing.

Four of Hearts

City Hall auditorium was almost full on the night we showed the movie. A whole bunch of people were there, including Jeanne Galletta, Flip, and, of course, Sam. But also people I didn't even know—from school and from around Hills Village.

Now that Clumsy Girl was "famous," people actually wanted to know more about the band. And they wanted to see the Rock-You-Mentary, too.

Mari, Nanci, and Patti all sat in different places in the auditorium. I had to stand up in front and say something before we started.

And the funny thing was, I didn't feel super-scared or nervous. I guess I was getting used to being in front of an audience. Or at least I had been, until our band dissolved into a puddle of disaster.

"Hi, everyone," I said. "Thanks for coming. We Stink is really proud of our Rock-You-Mentary and can't wait for you to see it. We're going to show the movie in just a minute, but I want to do one quick thing first."

Sam came over and set a stool down onstage and handed me my guitar. Rafe brought down the lights from the back. And then I started to play.

"This is for Mari, Patti, and Nanci," I said. "They'll know why."

I hadn't memorized the words to the song yet. It was still brand-new. So I had a cheat sheet on the floor in front of me, just in case.

But you know what? I didn't need it.

Because this song came straight from the heart.

Four of Hearts

I'm just one girl
With a guitar.
All by myself
Won't get too far.
But with you three
It's best, I think,
'Cause without you
I just can't stink.
A table falls
Without four legs.
A chicken needs
A dozen eggs.
A house can't stand
Without its walls.
I'll need you till
Niagara falls.
I never meant
To break the rules
But sometimes I'm
A big fat fool.
So listen, please,
And be my friend
And tell me:
Can We Stink again?

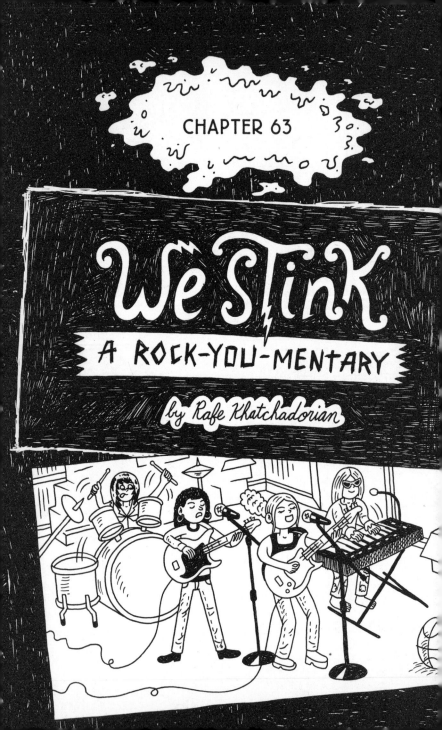

THE END

Dedicated to Flip Savage,
who took one for the team

Special thanks to Jeanne Galletta and Sam Marks

CHAPTER 64

Togetherness

The girls and I all hugged it out that night, and we even all stayed over at Mari's. It turned out they all missed the band as much as I did, but nobody wanted to be the first one to say it. I guess we were all just suddenly afraid of being honest with each other. And you can't be dishonest with your best friends. Which was just one more reason why I wasn't going to keep anything from them anymore.

And just to prove it, I let them read my whole journal. There wasn't anything about them in there, anyway. Just a bunch of really bad song ideas, and a couple of really good ones. And a whole lot of really weird doodles.

Which brings me to what happened next.

Mom says some guy named Andy Warhol once said that in the future, everyone will be famous for fifteen minutes. And even though Clumsy Girl lasted longer than that, she did go away after a while. Especially after some kid lost his pants when he fell into the monkey enclosure at the San Diego Zoo and racked up about a zillion hits. Poor kid. I know how he feels.

Meanwhile, now that Clumsy Girl and the Rock-You-Mentary had paved the way, We Stink was getting a whole bunch of new followers. And new requests, too.

We played at school again, and at the mall, and at Mari's dad's used car lot, and a whole bunch of birthday parties, too. We played new music, old music, and even learned some classic rock covers. We called the whole thing WE STINK: THE REUNION TOUR.

And it's still going strong.

By the Way

You're probably wondering what happened to Missy. That one's kind of complicated. We didn't call a truce or anything. It was more like...well, let's just say we're taking a break.

Should I have apologized to her for what I did? Yes and no, if you ask me. And that's where I was stuck.

I couldn't get Missy her phone back, but she couldn't get us another shot with Lulu, either.

And I don't think Missy saw it coming when I told her what *really* happened at the finals.

"If it wasn't for you, we wouldn't have given the best performance of our lives," I said.

"I'm getting uncomfortable now," Missy said.

"Don't worry, I'm not going to thank you," I told her.

"Good," she said, and we left it at that.

Will Missy and I ever get back together again? And by *get back together,* I mean will we go back to making each other's life miserable?

Maybe.

Well, probably.

Okay, almost definitely.

But in the meantime, I'm not going out of my way to pick any fights. In fact, I'm going to try to be more like Sam. He doesn't care about the Princesses either way. Maybe that makes him a geek in their eyes, but I think it's one of the coolest things about him.

And speaking of Sam...

Onward and Upward

When Mrs. Hibbs told Sam and me to stay after class, I thought it was because we'd been talking too much during her lecture.

But it wasn't anything like that.

"There's a regional competition for Rube Goldberg machines in Chicago this summer," she said. "I thought you two might be interested."

"What do we have to do?" Sam asked.

"Just build the best, most innovative machine you can think of," she said. "After that, the winners go on to the nationals in Washington, DC. But let's focus on one step at a time."

Sam looked at me like, *Are you thinking what I'm thinking?* And I looked back at him like, *I think I am.*

Then we both blurted it out at the same time. Except he said, "Windmill power!" And I said, "All the way to nationals!"

"Well, it sounds like you both bring something to the table." Mrs. Hibbs. said. "Now, if I could just get you to stop talking during class..."

We took a brochure to show our parents. And then out in the hall, we stopped by my locker to talk about it some more.

"This is going to take a lot of work," Sam said. "What about your band?"

"We're good," I said. "Once school's out, we'll have plenty of time for practicing and gigs."

"Very cool," Sam said. "So I guess we're doing this."

"I guess we are," I said, and we even shook on it.

Then we looked around to make sure Mrs. Stricker wasn't nearby, and we kissed on it, too. (Don't tell.)

We've got big plans now. And Mrs. Hibbs is right. Sam and I make a great team. This machine is going to be beyond awesome.

So watch out, Chicago, and watch out, world, because here I come!

Again.

About the Authors

JAMES PATTERSON received the Literarian Award for Outstanding Service to the American Literary Community from the National Book Foundation. He holds the Guinness World Record for the most #1 *New York Times* bestsellers, including *Max Einstein, Middle School, I Funny,* and *Jacky Ha-Ha,* and his books have sold more than 385 million copies worldwide. A tireless champion of the power of books and reading, Patterson created a children's book imprint, JIMMY Patterson, whose mission is simple: "We want every kid who finishes a JIMMY Book to say, 'PLEASE GIVE ME ANOTHER BOOK.'" He has donated more than one million books to students and soldiers and funds over four hundred Teacher Education Scholarships at twenty-four colleges and universities. He has also donated millions of dollars to independent bookstores and school libraries. Patterson invests proceeds from the sales of JIMMY Patterson Books in pro-reading initiatives.

CHRIS TEBBETTS has collaborated with James Patterson on eight books in the Middle School series and on *Public School Superhero,* and he is also the author of the Viking Saga, a fantasy adventure series for young readers. He lives in Vermont.

NEIL SWAAB is a New York City–based illustrator, designer, and author. His work has graced the covers and interiors of numerous books for children including his own series, The Secrets to Ruling School. He has also animated for TV and enjoys teaching at Parsons School of Design in the illustration program. Check out his work at neilswaab.com.

My name is Rafe Khatchadorian, and if there's one thing I know, it's how to stay out of trouble.

JUST KIDDING!

If you're in ~~jail~~ middle school now, or will be soon, my stories could help you survive. But even if they don't, you'll probably laugh your butt off reading about all my crazy adventures!

BUCKLE UP, FRIEND. WE'RE IN FOR A RIDE!

SLAM

rrroll

SPLAM!

Oscar couldn't believe he was hiking through the forest with a katt.

But, he figured he didn't have a choice. At least not until he was safely home, then he'd have all sorts of choices.

"This truce only lasts until we get back to base camp, right?" he said. "After that, I don't know you and you don't know me."

"Whatever," said Molly. "Let's head west."

Oscar grinned. He'd heard that katts could be

tricky. Sneaky, too. So, he'd do the exact opposite of whatever Molly suggested.

"Nope," he said. "We're going east."

"East? I've already been east. It's a waste of time. There's nothing there but a big cliff. I've seen it. Six different times!"

The katt knelt down on the trail and started scratching the dirt with her pointy claws. She gestured at Oscar's tattered uniform. "You're supposed to be a Dogg Scout, right?"

"Yes," Oscar said proudly. "I have fourteen merit badges. Most of them for chewing different things. Rope. Sticks. Squeak toys. Rawhide…"

"Well, let me draw you a map, Dogg Scout. East is the cliff. South, that's behind us, that's where the mountain lion likes to hang out."

Oscar nodded. He hated to admit it, but the katt was making sense.

"Okay, I've changed my mind," he announced. "We should go north or west."

"I choose west," said Molly.

"Sorry," said Oscar. "I don't really trust your

sense of direction. I, on the other hand, was a Dogg Scout. Obviously, I know more about what I'm doing than you do."

"Fine. Don't give yourself heartworms. We'll go north."

"Nope. West."

"West? That's what I said two minutes ago!"

"But I said it most recently. So, it's my idea."

Molly heaved a humongous sigh. "Fine. Whatever. Lead on."

Oscar trotted along the path, sniffing the breeze. No familiar scents tickled his nostrils.

After silently trudging through the wilderness, seeing nothing but trees and more trees, the two hikers finally came to a hilltop clearing.

"There!" Oscar panted. "That mountain! Way off in the distance! Do you see it?"

"Uh, yeah, Oscar," said Molly. "It's a mountain. Mountains are very hard *not* to see."

"I know that mountain!" said Oscar. "See how it looks like a huge hooked nose with a droopy wart on one side?"

"Yes," said Molly. "Sort of like your muzzle."

"That's not a wart on my muzzle," said Oscar, swiping his paw across his nose. "That's a booger. Anyway, I could see that exact same mountain from our campsite! It's what they call a landmark. Landmarks are good when you're lost. They mark the land for you!"

"Good work!" said Molly. "You're not as dumb as you look."

"Dumb? Hey, if I'm so dumb, how come I know

that katts have more than twenty muscles to control their ears? Too bad you don't have one to control your mouth!"

"Who studies katt muscles?" snarled the katt.

"A Dogg Scout working on his kattology merit badge, that's who!"

"Why would a dogg want to know so much about katts?"

Oscar didn't answer. His body went stiff. His eyes bugged out.

He raised one paw and pointed.

"Groundhog!"

And he took off running in the opposite direction.

Molly chased after the dogg who was chasing after a groundhog.

A naked groundhog. That meant it was one of the wild things living away from civilization.

"Did you get your rabies shot this year?" Molly hollered after Oscar. "Because if you didn't, that wild groundhog is going to give you one when it bites you in the butt! It's a wild creature, Oscar! Leave it alone."

"Can't," shouted Oscar. "It's a groundhog. I'm

a dogg. This is what they call instinct! A dogg's gotta do what a dogg's gotta do!"

"You're going to get us lost, again!" said Molly, trying to keep up with the dogg, who, she had to admit, was extremely athletic and could run very, very fast. "We're supposed to be hiking to the mountain. The one that's in the opposite direction of where you're chasing that groundhog!"

Just then, a flying squirrel flitted through the tree branches overhead.

"Squirrel!" shouted Oscar.

He dug in his paws, skidded to a stop, abandoned his wild groundhog chase, and took off after the flying squirrel.

"You are so like my brother!" cried Molly. "Blade would chase a reflection up a wall until he saw something shinier and then he'd chase after that!"

"I have to chase squirrels!" shouted Oscar. "Just like you have to spend your day unrolling toilet paper and climbing into cardboard boxes."

"I don't do that kitten stuff," said Molly

defensively. "Because I am no ordinary katt. I'm studying to be an actress!"

"Great," said Oscar, still running. "Give me a few lessons and I'll act like I'm interested."

He slammed on his brakes again.

"Oooh! Rabbit!"

He sped off in another completely random direction.

"Oscar?" pleaded Molly. "Forget the bunny rabbit. We need to hike to the mountain that looks like a hooked nose!"

"It'll still be there tomorrow. Mountains never move. But rabbits move fast! Very, very fast. This is excellent training for me. Coach will be so proud!"

"Please, Oscar! That mountain's five or ten miles away. We need to start walking to it immediately. We need to go back to the park. We need to find our families."

"Okay, okay," panted Oscar. "Rabbit's gone. No more distractions. Here I come."

Molly watched Oscar trot back to the hilltop.

"Sorry about that," said the dogg. "Instinct is a powerful thing, especially for athletic individuals such as myself. It kicks in, and *boom!*—It's like you're not in control of you anymore."

"If you say so," said Molly. "As an actress, I am much more in control of my emotions as well as my reactions."

That's when a butterfly flitted out of a patch of wildflowers.

Molly's tail sprang up. Her eyes bugged out.

"Butterfly!" she shouted.

"Whoa!" shouted Oscar. "Come back here! We're on a hike, remember?"

Molly ignored him and chased after the fluttering black and orange wings. She followed them into the forest and up a tree. Digging her claws into the bark she laddered up the towering evergreen effortlessly.

But then the butterfly drifted off into the open sky.

And Molly was stuck high up in the tree.

Katts are very good at climbing up trees. Climbing down from this height? Not so much.

Oscar perked up his ears.

Somewhere in the forest, a scaredy katt was yowling. Somewhere way up high.

He sniffed the wind.

Oh, yeah, he thought. *That's Molly.* He'd been smelling her all day. Her scent was permanently captured on his brain's internal memory chips.

Her yowls didn't sound so good. Oscar trotted along, underneath the trees, following her scent.

He came to the trunk of a tall pine and snorted along the bark.

This was the one. This was Molly's tree.

He tilted his head and looked up and up and up until he saw a lumpy shadow curled in a ball on one of the branches fifty feet above the forest floor.

"Molly?" he called out. "Is that you? It smells like you…"

"Yes, Oscar," came a faint reply. "It's me. I'm up a tree. Go ahead. Laugh."

"Okay. Ha, ha, ha." He paused. "Um, Molly?"

"What?" she shouted.

"What, exactly, am I laughing about?"

"Me! I'm stuck up a tree. Typical katt, right?"

"Yeah. It's because of your claws."

"What?"

"Katts can't climb down trees head-first because all the claws in your paws point toward your tail."

"Is that so?"

"Yeah. I told you: I'm working on my kattology merit badge. I know all sorts of katt stuff. For instance, katts walk like camels and giraffes: You move both of your right feet first, then you move both of your left feet."

"So, tell me something, brainiac: how do we katts climb *out* of a tree?"

"Very, very carefully," joked Oscar.

"Oscar?" Molly was sounding a little hissy. "You're not being very helpful."

"Sorry," said Oscar. "But climbing down is actually simple. Since your claws don't point the right way for a forward descent, all you have to do is *back* down the tree. At least that's what it said in the Dogg Scout Manual."

"You want me to back down the tree? Tail first?"

"Yup. Unless you want to stay up there and admire the view a little longer."

"No, thank you!"

"Then stick it in reverse!"

Oscar watched as Molly attempted to make her way, backward, down the tree.

Molly scuttled down ten feet, then stopped for a hiss break.

"Come on, katt!" urged Oscar. "You can do it!"

Molly inched down another two feet. A pair of birds on one of the branches was chirping at her.

"They're mocking me!" said Molly.

"They're mockingbirds," said Oscar. "It's what they do. Plus, once upon a time, somebody in your family probably ate one of their cousins. Come on. Quit having a hissy fit. Keep backing up."

Molly made it another five feet down the trunk.

"I can't do this!" she said, clinging onto the bark. "I tried, but I can't!"

"Fine," said Oscar. "Jump!"

"Jump?"

"It's only twenty more feet."

"Twenty feet?"

"Don't worry. I'll catch you."

"Promise?"

Oscar crossed his webbed toes behind his back. "Promise."

"All right. Here I come!"

Molly leapt from her perch. .

Oscar backed away from the tree.

Molly shrieked, spun around, shot out her legs, and crash-landed on all fours.

"That was awesome!" shouted Oscar, who found the frazzled look on Molly's frightened face to be funnier than anything he'd ever seen. "And hilarious!"

"Hilarious?" screeched Molly, narrowing her blue eyes. "I, for one, was not amused!"

"Oh, I knew you'd be okay," said Oscar. "You katts can spread out your legs like a parachute and land safely, even from way up high. For your information, there are katts who've survived falls from more than five hundred feet."

"And, for *your* information," hissed the katt, "there are many more who have suffered broken legs and worse falling out of a window or off a ladder!"

Oscar was dumbfounded. "Really?"

"Really!"

"Well, uh, they didn't mention that last bit in the Dogg Scout Manual…"

"Of course they didn't. A dogg wrote it! A dumb, ignorant, katt-hating dogg—just like you!"

READ MORE IN
KATT VS. DOGG,
AVAILABLE APRIL 2019!

1

The stench of horse manure woke Max Einstein with a jolt.

"Of course!"

Even though she was shivering, she threw off her blanket and hopped out of bed. Actually, it wasn't really a bed. More like a lumpy, water-stained mattress with frayed seams. But that didn't matter. Ideas could come wherever they wanted.

She raced down the dark hall. The floorboards—bare planks laid across rough beams—creaked and wobbled with every step. Her red hair, of course, was a bouncing tangle of wild curls. It was always a bouncing tangle of wild curls.

Max rapped her knuckles on a lopsided door hanging off rusty hinges.

"Mr. Kennedy?" She knocked again. "Mr. Kennedy?"

"What the…" came a sleepy mumble. "Max? Are you okay?"

Max took that question as permission to enter Mr. Kennedy's apartment. She practically burst through his wonky door.

"I'm fine, Mr. Kennedy. In fact, I'm better than fine! I've got something great here! At least I think it's something great. Anyway, it's really, really cool. This idea could change everything. It could save our world. It's what Mr. Albert Einstein would've called an 'aha' moment."

"Maxine?"

"Yes, Mr. Kennedy?"

"It's six o'clock in the morning, girl."

"Is it? Sorry about the inconvenient hour. But you never know when a brainstorm will strike, do you?"

"No. Not with *you,* anyway…"

Max was wearing a floppy trench coat over her shabby sweater. Lately, she'd been sleeping in the sweater under a scratchy horse blanket because her so-called bedroom was, just like Mr. Kennedy's, extremely cold.

The tall and sturdy black man, his hair flecked with patches of white, creaked out of bed and rubbed some of the sleep out of his eyes. He slid his bare feet into shoes he had fashioned out of cardboard and old newspapers.

"Hang on," he said. "Need to put on my bedroom slippers here…"

"Because the floor's so cold," said Max.

"Huh?"

"You needed to improvise those bedroom slippers because the floor's cold every morning. Correct?"

"Maxine—we're sleeping, uninvited, above a horse stable. Of course the floors are cold. And, in case you haven't noticed, the place doesn't smell so good, either."

Max, Mr. Kennedy, and about a half-dozen other homeless people were what New York City called "squatters." That meant they were living rent-free in the vacant floors above a horse stable. The first two floors of the building housed a parking garage for Central Park carriages and stalls for the horses that pulled them. The top three floors? As far as the owner of the building knew, they were vacant.

"Winter is coming, Mr. Kennedy. We have no central heating system."

"Nope. We sure don't. You know why? Because we don't pay rent, Max!"

"Be that as it may, in the coming weeks, these floors will only become colder. Soon, we could all freeze to death. Even if we were to board up all the windows—"

"That's not gonna happen," said Mr. Kennedy. "We

need the ventilation. All that horse manure downstairs, stinking up the place…"

"Exactly! That's precisely what I wanted to talk to you about. That's my big idea. *Horse manure!*"

2

"It's simple, really, Mr. Kennedy," said Max, moving to the cracked plaster wall and finding a patch that wasn't covered with graffiti.

She pulled a thick stub of chalk out her baggy sweater pocket and started sketching on the wall, turning it into her blackboard.

"Please hear me out, sir. Try to see what I see."

Max, who enjoyed drawing in a beat-up sketchbook she rescued from a Dumpster, chalked in a lump of circles radiating stink marks. She labeled it "manure/biofuel."

"To stay warm this winter, all we have to do is arrange a meeting with Mr. Sammy Monk."

"The owner of this building?" said Mr. Kennedy,

skeptically. "The landlord who doesn't even know we're here? *That* Mr. Sammy Monk?"

"Yes, sir," said Max, totally engrossed in the diagram she was drafting on the wall. "We need to convince him to let us have all of his horse manure."

Mr. Kennedy stood up. "All of his manure? Now why on earth would we want that, Max? It's manure!"

"Well, once we have access to the manure, I will design and engineer a green gas mill for the upstairs apartments."

"A green what mill?"

"Gas, sir. We can rig up an anaerobic digester that will turn the horse manure into biogas, which we can then combust to generate electricity and heat."

"You want to burn horse manure gas?"

"Exactly! Anaerobic digestion is a series of biological processes in which microorganisms break down biodegradable material, such as horse manure, in the absence of oxygen, which is what 'anaerobic' means. That's the solution to our heating and power problems."

"You sure you're just twelve years old?"

"Yes. As far as I know."

Mr. Kennedy gave Max a look that she, unfortunately, was used to seeing. The look said she was crazy. Nuts. Off her rocker. But Max never let "the look" upset her. It was like Albert Einstein said, "Great spirits have always encountered violent opposition from mediocre minds."

Not that Mr. Kennedy had a mediocre mind. Max just wasn't doing a good enough job explaining her bold new breakthrough idea. Sometimes, the ideas came into her head so fast they came out of her mouth in a mumbled jumble.

"All we need, Mr. Kennedy, is an airtight container— something between the size of an oil drum and a tanker truck." She sketched a boxy cube fenced in by a pen of steel posts. "Heavy plastic would be best, of course. And it would be good if it had a cage of galvanized iron bars surrounding it. Then we just have to measure and cut three different pipes—one for feeding in the manure, one for the gas outlet, and one for displaced liquid fertilizer. We would insert these conduits into the tank through a universal seal, hook up the appropriate plumbing, and we'd be good to go."

Mr. Kennedy stroked his stubbly chin and admired Max's detailed design of the device sketched on the flaking wall.

"A brilliant idea, Max," he said. "Like always."

Max allowed herself a small, proud smile.

"Thank you, Mr. Kennedy."

"Slight problem."

"What's that, sir?"

"Well, that container there. The cube. That's what? Ten feet by ten feet by ten feet?"

"About."

"And you say you need a cage of bars around it. You also mentioned three pipes. And plumbing. Then I figure you're going to need a furnace to burn the horse manure gas, turn it into heat."

Max nodded. "And a generator. To spin our own electricity."

"Right. Won't that cost a whole lot of money?"

Max lowered her chalk. "I suppose so."

"And have you ever noticed the one thing most people squatting in this building don't have?"

Max pursed her lips. "Money?"

"Uhm-hmm. Exactly."

Max tucked the stubby chalk back into her sweater pocket and dusted off her pale, cold hands.

"Point taken, Mr. Kennedy. As usual, I need to be more practical. I'll get back to you with a better plan. I'll get back to you before winter comes."

"Great. But, Max?"

"Yes, sir?"

Mr. Kennedy climbed back into his lumpy bed and pulled up the blanket.

"Just don't get back to me before seven o'clock, okay?"

3

Max glanced at her watch.

It was only 6:17 a.m. She, unlike Mr. Kennedy, was an early riser. Always had been, probably always would be. The morning, especially that quiet space between dreaming and total wakefulness, was when most of her massive ideas floated through her drowsy brain. The ideas helped tamp down the sadness that could come in those same quiet times. A sadness that all orphans probably shared. Made more intense because Max had no idea who either of her parents were.

Max creaked her way back up the hall to her room as quietly as she could. She could hear Mr. Kennedy already snoring behind her.

Max had decorated her own sleeping space in the stables

building the same way she had decorated all the rooms she had ever temporarily lived in: by propping open her battered old suitcase on its side to turn it into a display case for all things Albert Einstein. Books by and about the famous scientist were lined along the bottom like a bookshelf. Both lids were filled with her collection of Einstein photographs and quotes. She even had an Einstein bobblehead doll she'd found, once upon a time, in a museum store dumpster. She used it as a bookend.

Max couldn't remember where the suitcase came from. She'd just always had it. It was older than her rumpled knit sweater, and that thing was an antique.

The oldest photograph in her collection, the one that someone other than Max (she didn't know who) had pasted inside the suitcase lid so long ago that its edges were curling, showed the great professor lost in thought. He had a bushy mustache and long, unkempt hair. His hands were clasped together, almost as if in prayer. His eyes were gazing up toward infinity.

That photograph was Max's oldest memory. And since she never knew her own parents, at an early age, Max found herself talking to the kind, grandfatherly man at bedtime. He was a very good listener. She became curious as to who the mystery man might be, and that's how her lifelong infatuation with all things Einstein began.

Like how he was born in Germany but had to leave his home before the Second World War. And how he was so busy thinking of big, amazing ideas, he sometimes forgot to pay attention to his job at the patent office. They had a lot in common.

Next to the photograph was Max's absolute favorite Einstein quote: "Imagination is more important than knowledge."

"Unless, of course, you don't have the money to make the things you dream up come true," Max muttered.

Mr. Kennedy was right.

She couldn't afford to build her green gas mill. And she couldn't ask Mr. Sammy Monk for his horse manure or anything else because Mr. Sammy Monk couldn't know anybody was living in the abandoned floors of his horse stable. She'd just have to imagine a different solution to the squatters' heating dilemma. One that didn't cost a dime and could be created out of someone else's discarded scraps.

Max turned to her computer, which she had built herself from found parts. It was amazing what some people in New York City tossed to the curb on garbage pickup days. Max had been able to solder together (with a perfectly good soldering iron someone had thrown out) enough discarded circuit boards, unwanted wiring, abandoned processors, rejected keyboards, and one slightly blemished retina screen from a cast-off MacBook Pro to create a machine that whirred even faster than her mind.

She also had free wi-fi, thanks to the Link NYC public hot spot system. She could even recharge her computer's batteries (discovered abandoned behind one of the city's glossy Apple stores) at the kiosk just down the block from the stables. (Reliable wi-fi was one of the main reasons Max had selected her current accommodations. Easy access to a top-flight school was the other.)

Max clicked open a browser and went back to the internet page she had bookmarked the night before.

It was a nightmarish news report about children as young as seven "working in perilous conditions in the Democratic Republic of the Congo to mine cobalt that ends up in smartphones, cars, and computers sold to millions across the world." The children, as many as forty thousand, were being paid one dollar a day to do backbreaking work. They were also helping make a shadowy international business consortium called the Corp very, very, *very* rich.

The story broke Max's heart.

Because Max's heart, like her hero Dr. Einstein's, was huge.

4

Max was packing her bookbag for school when she heard a commotion down on the street.

She dropped her backpack and raced to the nearest dirt-smeared window to peer through a hole in the glass.

She saw two police cars. Their roof bar lights were swirling. Even from four stories up, Max could hear snatches of orders crackling out of the cruiser's dashboard radio: "Squatters…eviction…arrest…trespassing…"

Then she saw two officers, a man and a woman, escorting Mrs. Rabinowitz—a sweet widow who lived on the third floor—out of the building and toward their police car. Mrs. Rabinowitz's frumpy housecoat was flapping in the breeze, exposing her knee-high stockings.

"There're more squatters upstairs," said the female cop. "We may need backup."

"On it," said a cop, casually leaning up against one of the cruisers with a radio mic in his hand. He seemed to be the man in charge. "Yeah, this is Alpha Three Five Oh," he said matter-of-factly into his microphone. "One suspect in custody. More in building. Request backup."

Max had heard enough.

She raced down four flights of steep, switchback staircases and into the bright morning light.

"Excuse me, officers," she said, holding up a hand to shield her eyes from the sun. "Might I have a word?"

"What? Who are you, kid?" asked the cop who seemed to be in charge.

"Maxine Einstein, sir."

"Like the egghead Einstein? The E equals M-C squared guy?"

Max didn't answer. Instead, she tried to keep the conversation focused and on point. She had learned long ago that it was hard to achieve your desired scientific outcome if you let your mind wander into trivialities.

"Why are you arresting Mrs. Rabinowitz?" she asked, her voice strong and firm.

"Because, little Miss Einstein, your friend here is a squatter. She can't live in this building without paying rent.

Neither can any of those other people upstairs." The police officer gave Max a menacing look. "Neither can you, kid."

"Officer, if I may, are you familiar with the legal term 'adverse possession'?"

"Oh. So now you're a little lawyer?"

"No, officer. I have not completed the necessary course of study, nor have I passed the New York State bar exam. However, I do know that adverse possession is the legal term for occupying someone else's property. When you do so, you obtain what are known as 'squatter's rights.' In the state of New York, a person has to live on the property openly and without permission of the owner for a period of at least ten uninterrupted years to be able to claim adverse possession."

"You telling me these folks have been squatting over Mr. Monk's stables for more than ten years and he just now called us about it?"

"No. I believe the squatters have only been in possession of this particular premises for six or seven months. I will have to check with Mr. Kennedy for specifics."

"Well, little Miss Einstein, six or seven months isn't ten years."

"True. However, in New York *City* the laws are different than they are in New York *State*. We have our own set of adverse possession laws, which you, of course, are sworn to uphold. In New York City, sir, a person is granted squatter's rights after just thirty days."

The cop stared at Max with a blank expression on his face. She often had that effect on people.

"After thirty days," she continued, "a New York City squatter has the right to continue living in a building until the actual owner—in this case, Mr. Sammy Monk—goes through the lengthy and, I am told, very expensive process of legal eviction. From my understanding, that can take up to a year. Sometimes longer."

The other police officers were now staring at the one holding the radio microphone, wondering what to do next. Two of them still had their hands gripped on Mrs. Rabinowitz's arms, waiting for orders.

The officer in charge shook his head.

"Let her go."

The other officers did.

Mrs. Rabinowitz rubbed her arms where the police had been clutching them and hurried over to Max to give her a kiss.

"Thank you, dear," she whispered.

"You're welcome, Mrs. Rabinowitz. Glad I could be of assistance."

"I found a bagel with cream cheese yesterday. Want it?"

"No, thank you, Mrs. Rabinowitz. I already ate breakfast."

"Good. It's the most important meal of the day…"

The frail widow scurried back into the stables.

"Hey, Einstein?" said the lead cop.

"Yes, sir?"

"What school do you go to? I wanna send my son there."

5

Max ran upstairs to grab her backpack.

The discussion with the police officer had knocked her off her very rigid schedule.

She had to force herself to stay organized—not always easy when you're absentminded and prone to what Mr. Kennedy called "too much daydreaming." He thought you should only dream while you were asleep. "You know—nightdreaming!"

But Max didn't have a mother or father to tell her when it was time to wake up, go to bed, do her homework, eat her vegetables, turn off the TV, or hurry because she'd miss the subway if she didn't. Max was completely on her own.

Well, not completely. She had Mr. Kennedy, Mrs. Rabinowitz, and the other squatters in the building. But, to be honest, none of them really possessed what Max would call "stellar time-management skills."

But they loved her and she loved them back. That was good enough for Max. The homeless people camping out above the stables were the closest thing she'd had to family in a long time. Max didn't even know if "Einstein" was her real family name. Was she related to the famous genius?

She didn't know.

Max Einstein had no idea who she was, where she came from, how she ended up in New York City, or where she got the name Max Einstein. She liked to think of it as the one great mystery in life that she couldn't begin to solve, especially not today. She was running late (even for her).

"Have a good day at school, Max!" Mrs. Rabinowitz cried out as Max bounded down the staircase to the third floor.

"Thank you!"

"You sure you don't want half of this bagel? It's got *strawberry* cream cheese."

"No, thanks. Gotta run."

She made it to the main floor of the stables. "Morning, Domino, Kit Kat, and Opie!" she cried.

The horses whinnied in their stalls and flicked their tails.

"Keep making manure, guys," said Max. "One day, we're going to build that green gas mill!"

The day after I win the lottery, she thought.

The horse stables were on the western edge of Manhattan, close to the Hudson River. Max had to dash four blocks east and a couple blocks south to take the downtown subway at West 50th Street and Eighth Avenue.

She caught a lucky break. A train screeched into the station just as she hurdled down the steps. Max leaped through the doors, which were closing like a hungry steel mouth, and tumbled into the crowded car.

"Sorry," she said, as she bumped into a clump of commuters clutching a pole. She found a handhold just before the train lurched forward. When it did, she fell slightly backward because of, well, physics. Sir Isaac Newton, the granddaddy of modern physics, developed laws of motion, including the one that says a body at rest tends to stay at rest—even when a train accelerated forward.

That's exactly what Max's body (and all the other bodies crammed into the rush hour train) did. When the train came to a stop, they would all lurch forward because, by then, their bodies would be in motion and tending to stay in motion.

While the subway car rocked south at thirty miles per hour, Max observed a fly zipping through the car, headed north.

So how fast is the fly flying? she wondered with a grin. *It's all relative, of course.*

That was one of Albert Einstein's most famous ideas: the theory of relativity.

How fast the fly was flying *uptown* on a subway car hurtling *downtown* depended on how you measured things. It was all *relative* to your perspective.

The fly was, simultaneously, going five miles per hour in one direction and twenty-five in the other.

Someone standing in the subway tunnel as the train rumbled past (a very dumb idea, especially for a scientist) would measure the fly's speed as moving *south* at twenty-five miles per hour.

But, inside the car, Max perceived it as moving five miles per hour *north*.

Until a big guy, two poles up, plucked the poor little bug out of the air in mid-flight and smooshed it.

Then it wasn't moving at all.

6

Nine minutes later, Max emerged from the West 4th Street station and glanced at her watch.

She was back on schedule. She saw some kids playing a frantic game of pickup basketball, their bookbags leaning up against the chain-link fence penning in the court. She wondered what that would be like. To play on the way to school. Max didn't spend much time with other children. There weren't very many in her world. In a weird way, Albert Einstein was probably her best friend.

As she walked along, she noticed all sorts of things that reminded her of Einstein's incredible contributions to the modern world—if only he were alive to see them.

She saw a tourist couple consulting a map app on their smartphone. The app, of course, relied on GPS to pinpoint their precise location on the island of Manhattan. It bounced a signal off satellites orbiting the Earth. The app could help them find the nearest Starbucks with GPS, which worked because of Einstein's theory of relativity and something he called *time dilation*. Smartphones were smart because Einstein was smarter.

Max glanced at her watch. She had time to stop by Washington Square Park and see if Mr. Weinstock was interested in a quick game of speed chess.

Mr. Leonard "Lenny" Weinstock claimed to be from London, England. Max was never certain if he was telling her the truth about that. Or the fact that he graduated from Oxford. Or that he met the queen. "On several different occasions, mind you."

Max just knew he was a nice old man with a very proper British accent who always wore checked shirts, a safari vest, and a flat cap—the kind cabbies used to wear. Mr. Weinstock also liked to play chess as much as Max did.

"Ah, good morning, Maxine," he said when Max plopped down on the bench opposite him at one of the park's many outdoor chess tables.

"Good morning, Mr. Weinstock."

"Care for a game?"

"Yes, sir. If you're up for it."

"Of course, dear. I believe you're currently ahead in our ongoing tally of pairings."

"Yes, sir. Slightly."

In truth, Max had won far more games against Mr. Weinstock than she had lost. And the ones she did lose, she lost on purpose. There really was no need to crush Mr. Weinstock's fighting spirit with a string of unrelenting defeats. As it was, he was just about the only regular in Washington Square Park who was willing to play against Max Einstein. Her reputation preceded her.

"Blitz, bullet, or lightning?" asked Mr. Weinstock, referring to the various levels of speed chess.

"Is lightning okay today?" asked Max. "I don't want to be late for school."

"Right you are. Lightning it is, then."

Mr. Weinstock bopped a button on top of a digital timer. Each player would have ten seconds to ponder and make their moves.

"Checkmate," said Max after five moves. "Sorry about that, Mr. Weinstock. I'm sure you'll beat me next time when we'll both have time to think through our moves more carefully."

Mr. Weinstock chuckled. "Yes, Max. I'm certain we'll *both* enjoy having more time for leisurely contemplation. Have a good day at school, dear."

"Thank you, sir."

Max hurried off, promising herself that, the next time they played, she'd definitely let Mr. Weinstock win.

Fortunately, her school was very close to Washington Square Park.

Because, even though she was only twelve, Max Einstein was already going to college—at New York University!